Jed's attention focused on her.

Those dark eyes seemed to peer into her innermost part. Her breath caught for a moment. She felt a warmth and a curiosity that surprised her. What was there about this man that caught her unaware?

Laura blinked. She could almost feel the energy radiating from Jed. The focus on her was unsettling. He was not at all like Jordan, despite his looks. She'd do well not to confuse the two just because they looked identical....

BARBARA McMAHON

The Forbidden Brother

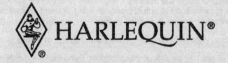

TORONTO • NEW YORK • LONDON
AMSTERDAM • PARIS • SYDNEY • HAMBURG
STOCKHOLM • ATHENS • TOKYO • MILAN • MADRID
PRAGUE • WARSAW • BUDAPEST • AUCKLAND

ISBN-13: 978-0-373-03963-0
ISBN-10:   0-373-03963-8

THE FORBIDDEN BROTHER

First North American Publication 2007.

Copyright © 2007 by Barbara McMahon.

www.eHarlequin.com

Printed in U.S.A.

Barbara McMahon was born and raised in the American South, but settled in California after spending a year flying around the world for an international airline. After settling down to raise a family and work for a computer firm, she began writing when her children started school. Now, feeling fortunate in being able to realize a long-held dream of quitting her "day job" and writing full-time, she and her husband have moved to the Sierra mountains of California, where she finds her desire to write is stronger than ever. With the beauty of the mountains visible from her windows, and the pace of life slower than the hectic San Francisco Bay Area where they previously resided, she finds more time than ever to think up stories and characters and share them with others through writing.

Barbara loves to hear from readers. You can reach her at P.O. Box 977, Pioneer, CA 95666-0977, USA. Readers can also contact Barbara at her Web site: www.barbaramcmahon.com.

CHAPTER ONE

LAURA carefully replaced the receiver of the phone. She wanted to slam it down after first yelling at Maria Brodie to stop calling her every day in her attempts to micromanage everything. But discretion being the better part of business life, she had kept her voice calm, sharing none of her frustration with the woman on the other end of the line. Proud of her self-control, she waited until the connection had been cut before giving a discreet *"Eeeek!"*

The woman drove her crazy!

Not for the first time since Hugo Atkins had died, Laura wished he was still running the gallery and the one she could escalate problems to. But the buck stopped with her these days. Inheriting the small art gallery in Miragansett turned out to be a mixed blessing. Normally she loved her calling, even when dealing with difficult artists like Maria Brodie. Actually if Laura and Maria's conversation had centered around Maria's work, it would have been easier to deal with.

Instead they were involved in an ongoing battle to determine how many of Maria's son's paintings would be displayed in a public retrospective Laura had agreed to host at the gallery next month. They were in the final stages of planning, only two weeks left before the night of the opening. Laura wished Maria would let her do what she did well and go back to her painting.

She leaned back in her chair, rubbing her temples. She was getting a headache as she often did after dealing with the temperamental artist. Some of it was pure guilt. Keeping a life-changing secret wasn't easy. At one point, Laura had expected Maria to become her mother-in-law. Now she wondered if they could have been so related and not end up killing each other one day. It was hard enough dealing with her since Jordan died. Her own emotions were in turmoil. The hurt and grief was gradually easing. Dealing with Maria kept everything to the forefront. She hoped time would heal the relationship. Once the show was over, there'd be little necessity of daily checkups by Maria. Come on July!

"Laura, I need you out here right away!" her assistant called from the gallery.

Heather was usually a calm and collected young woman. What caused that note of panic in her voice?

Was there an emergency? Laura rose and dashed across her small, cluttered office. Off-limits to all but closest friends or business associates, the office reflected none of the serenity and beauty of the displays in the gallery. Stacks of papers cluttered the desk. A utilitarian file cabinet sat against one wall. The furnishings were functional and serviceable, nothing fancy. Hugo had left all that to the showrooms of the gallery.

She opened the door and stepped into another world. Paintings graced the walls, discreetly illuminated by full spectrum, high tech lights. Thick carpeting muffled most sounds. Scattered artfully on free-standing pedestals were sculptures of renown. She offered metal, stone and glass objets d'art, as well as the paintings for which the gallery was known. Hugo had built the business in the historic Cape Cod town to cater to locals and tourists alike. Laura was carrying on in his footsteps.

Heather stood across the room talking to a tall man whose back was toward Laura. He wore a business suit, unusual during the casual summer months. The expression on her assistant's face was indescribable. When she spotted Laura, relief became evident. The man turned.

Laura stopped—stunned. Her heart caught in her throat. It was impossible. Before her stood Jordan Brodie! A thrill of gladness swept through her for a split second.

Then the truth hit her. This couldn't be Jordan—she'd attended his funeral three months ago.

"Laura Parkerson?" the man asked. The voice wasn't Jordan's. It sounded different, more clipped, not as lazy and teasing. The expression on his face was mingled: wariness and cynicism. Yet he looked exactly like Jordan.

"Yes?"

"You own this gallery?" he asked.

"I do."

"I thought it belonged to Hugo Atkins."

"It did. He died a couple of years ago. Now it's mine." No need to go into the details of her inheritance. She'd worked for Hugo for several years, learned so much from him. She missed him every day. He knew she loved the place as much as he had and, with no children to inherit, he'd made Laura his heir.

"He's Jordan's brother," Heather said needlessly. "His twin brother."

"I didn't know—" Laura started to say. She closed her mouth. Why should she be surprised to discover her former fiancé's brother was a *twin*. It was not the first thing Jordan had kept from her. Once again the sadness of her loss swept through her. She'd loved him. To her Jordan had hung the moon. Until that fateful day. She rubbed her chest, the ache as fresh as it had been three months ago when she'd learned of Jordan's betrayal and death.

"What can I do for you?" Seeing him was like seeing a slightly skewed version of Jordan. This man was the same size and shape, but there was an electricity about him that never came from Jordan. An assurance that came from a quiet self-confidence, not arrogance from bravado and posturing. Jordan had been as charming as could be, which allowed him to get away with things other men couldn't. And allowed him to sweep her off her feet. She'd never felt so special as when she'd been with Jordan Brodie.

"I'm Jed Brodie. I've come to pick up my brother's paintings. I understand you have some of them," he said.

"I do. I just got off the phone with your mother, as a matter of fact. We're working on the scheduling of a retrospective for his work next month. What do you mean you've come to pick up the paintings? I'll be framing them here. Is that a problem?"

"I need to get the paintings appraised for tax purposes. And if they're worth anything, decide if I want to sell them now or later." He glanced at his watch impatiently.

"Sell them?" Laura felt like a parrot. But she didn't understand. Was he expecting some kind of windfall from Jordan's body of work? "Your mother said she didn't want the paintings sold. She wants to show them to the community as a memorial to Jordan." The problem was Maria wanted to show them all. Laura was hard-pressed to pick a dozen or so to fit in the alcove where the display would be.

She glanced at the alcove. Jordan had pushed her for an exhibit in her gallery from the day he met her. Fully convinced he would set the art world on fire, he'd been relentless in pushing to have a one-man show. She'd been equally reluctant. She didn't like mixing business and personal. Plus, sad to say, Jordan's work wasn't the high caliber she was used to showing. Maybe if he'd worked harder at it. Forever too late now.

"My mother has little say in the matter. I need to find out what they are worth and then dispose of them—either sell, give away or toss in the trash, whatever's appropriate."

"These are your brother's paintings. You can't throw them away." Laura was horrified at the thought. She knew the paintings would never be classified as great works, but wasn't there any family loyalty and ties? The two men were twins, for heaven's sake. Weren't twins supposed to be close?

He looked down his nose at her obviously not wishing to belabor the subject. "Actually I can do whatever I want with them."

"But I've already scheduled the showing. Announcements have been made in all the local papers. The brochures are at the printer's just waiting the final details. Framing has started. You can't halt everything at this point." Did he have any idea of how much work she'd already done?

"Then perhaps you and I need to discuss the matter before things proceed any further. I'm only here for a few days. I need to get everything lined up and taken care of before I leave," he said impatiently.

"Your brother died three months ago and you're just showing up now?" No one had said a word about Jordan's brother at the funeral. She thought it odd, but her own grief and guilt kept her from questioning anything too closely.

Why had he arrived today? And what business was it of his what happened to Jordan's paintings? Maria was definite with her plans. She wanted her son to have his day in the sun, even if posthumously.

He glanced at Heather, then back at Laura. "Is there some-place we can discuss this in private?"

Laura hesitated. She felt like she was in a time warp, talking to Jordan, only not. Staring at Jordan and seeing someone different. Feeling mingled emotions, longing for what was long gone; confusion as she noted the differences between the men. A little animosity flared at his attitude and his threats to her carefully planned show. An acute awareness of the man's mas-culinity surprised her.

He was obviously Jordan's identical twin, but neither Jordan nor his parents had ever mentioned that fact to her. All Jordan had ever said was his younger brother rarely came home. How much younger could a twin be?

"Are you the black sheep of the family?" she blurted out. Maria and Jefferson Brodie had talked a little about this son. Once Maria had said he'd gone off to do his own thing and turned his back on his family. He wasn't interested in painting or sculpturing. And from what Laura knew of the family, they had no interest in anything that did not center around painting or sculpturing.

"If you call getting a good education and then supporting myself by working, then yeah, I guess you could say that," he replied.

It was in direct contrast to Jordan. He'd dropped out of college to paint. The call of his muse, he'd often said. And paint he did, when the mood struck. The rest of the time, he spent on other pursuits. But none that entailed a nine-to-five job. He was usually seeking inspiration by lying on the beach, sailing or clubbing.

Their mother, Maria Brodie, was a famous oil painter. Her works brought tens of thousands of dollars with each sale. Jefferson Brodie was the father of the Brodie men, an extraordinary sculptor whose marble and granite creations she'd love to represent, but who had an exclusive deal with a Manhattan agency.

Maria did condescend to sell some of her paintings through her gallery, not as many as Laura might wish for, but probably more than she should expect given how limited her clientele was.

From the first moment Laura met Jordan, she'd known Maria expected her son to follow in her footsteps. Yet, not for her precious son the struggles of a starving artist. She supplied the cottage he lived in and support while he painted. Even the flashy car that he'd wrapped around a very unforgiving tree had come from his mother.

Jordan had painted, partied and left a collection of work some of which Laura was going to show in memory of a man who died too young.

Now this man, Jordan's own brother, threatened those plans. She needed to talk to him and he was right, darn him, the showroom wasn't the place.

"Come with me. Heather, handle anything that comes up, will you?" Laura headed for the workshop in the back of the gallery, where Jordan's paintings awaited framing. The warehouselike space was lined with shelves holding different paintings or sculptures. Some were awaiting display. Others had been bought and would be shipped to their new owners in the next day or two.

Frames leaned against one wall, an assortment of sizes and styles used to enhance any work she displayed to make it more appealing to the buyer. Some frames were for sale, others were merely for display use while a painting was on exhibit. Large worktables were as cluttered with paraphernalia as her office. Yet she knew where everything was. The layout suited her perfectly.

Laura held open the door while Jed Brodie stepped inside and looked around. She followed and closed the door to the gallery, leaning against it. She wasn't sure what to expect. Certainly not the image of Jordan looking at her with impatience. Jordan would have tried to sweet-talk her into whatever scheme he had come up with. Kisses would go a long way to have her fall in with his plans. For a moment, she missed the love they'd shared—that she'd thought they'd shared.

This man looked coldly around the space and didn't say a word. She would not take offense, though she could feel herself bristle a little in defense of her workshop. But there would be no cajoling, no teasing, no kisses. He looked hard as iron.

Jed turned and faced her. "I understand you were Jordan's fiancée," he said, glancing at her from head to toe.

She felt like a display piece. One he would not wish to purchase.

She nodded watching him warily. For a moment she felt a pang that she had not even known his name. How awful to have a family who disregarded a son so completely. If his assessment was to be believed, he didn't fit the role of black sheep. He looked dynamic and successful. She had a good eye for fine things and the suit and shoes he wore were fine indeed. His hair was cut shorter than Jordan's and his eyes were clear and sharp.

She took a breath in surprise when that smidge of interest didn't dissipate. It was totally unwanted. He wasn't Jordan. She shook off the momentary lapse. She'd had enough dealings with the Brodies. The sooner this one was gone, the better.

"We were engaged," she acknowledged. "He told me once he had a brother who was off building bridges. Since he never mentioned another brother, I assume that's you."

"Probably all he told you. I'm an engineer, and yes, I build bridges in places of the world where transportation means the difference between living and dying for entire villages."

"That could be said for anywhere. All goods have to be transported."

"True, but where I was working was out of the normal travel lanes. The message about his death didn't reach me until last week. It's taken me this long to get here."

"Last week? He died three months ago. Your office didn't notify you?" She couldn't believe a telegram or e-mail or something hadn't gotten through earlier than last week. Despite not wanting to feel anything for the man, she felt a touch of regret that he'd just learned of his brother's death. It had to have hit hard.

"Have you dealt with my parents much?" Jed asked.

"Primarily your mother. She lets me sell some of her work." She would not tell him how Maria was driving her crazy about the showing of Jordan's work. She was Jed's mother, as well, and Laura believed in being discreet. Wasn't that the reason she never told what she'd discovered that last day? She wanted to spare Maria the heartache. And herself the embarrassment, if she were honest.

She wished she'd not known. That Jordan had gone to his grave with the secret and she could mourn him with all the passion she held for him.

"She called the home office and left word for me to call. Nothing more. Nothing to indicate that it was a family emergency, not that there had been a death in the family. The message about the call came in my regular mail, which I get about every three to four months, unless it's critical, in which case it's faxed or e-mailed."

From the tight control he exercised, she suspected he was furious with the situation. She'd always heard twins had a close connection. How sad to lose his brother and then not find out for three months. Maria wouldn't have done it deliberately, she knew. The woman lived in her own world. Surfacing occasionally to interact with others, then going back to the paintings she did so brilliantly.

"So when I returned her call last week, she told me," he ended bleakly.

"I'm so sorry," she said, her heart going out to him. Despite everything, she'd loved Jordan and could relate to how his brother must be feeling.

He ignored her offer of sympathy. "Where are the paintings?"

She went to the rack where she had them stacked. To an outsider, it might look haphazardly arranged, but she knew exactly where everything was. The large room was climate controlled, necessary in the salty air of Cape Cod and the humidity of summer. The floor was immaculate. The paintings were arranged by subject matter. She gestured to the facing one.

Jed studied it a moment, then looked at her.

"What's its value?"

Was that all he cared about? Money? "I haven't appraised the lot. Your mother said she only wanted them on display, not appraised."

"Well, my mother lives in her own world. What price would you list it for in the show?"

"Actually the show is a retrospective. Your parents did not plan to sell any paintings. I thought your mother wished to keep his work."

He reached into an inner coat pocket and pulled out a bulging envelope. He held it out for her. "You'll see Jordan left me in charge of his estate. According to his attorney, I have complete authority. And I don't have time to wait around for several weeks while you show his paintings and then decide what the next step is. I have a bridge halfway built. I want to liquidate the assets and divide them among the family members, as he indicated. Then I need to get back to work."

Laura looked at the envelope and then at him. "So leave the paintings in my hands and I'll tell you how the showing goes," she said flippantly. "Your mother really wants this for Jordan." Laura hoped giving the exhibit would ease some of her own grief at the way things turned out.

Jed studied the painting for a minute. "Is it any good?"

Laura looked at it. "It will appeal to a certain portion of the population," she said carefully.

"Like some farmer in Iowa?" he said derisively.

She looked at him in surprise. Did he know she was from Iowa? Was that a criticism on her judgment?

"I may not be artistic, but I can recognize excellent work. My mother's paintings have a depth that's amazing and a use of color that's phenomenal. This looks like a paint-by-numbers view of a ubiquitous Cape Cod seascape," he continued.

Laura bit her lip in indecision. Normally she agreed with customers—it went a long way to selling art. Agreement with the artists kept them happy and kept them bringing in more work. She didn't like confrontation. But this was different.

"Am I wrong?" he challenged. His dark eyes so like yet unlike Jordan's, held hers.

"No," she admitted reluctantly. "But there's a definite market from tourists who want souvenirs to remind them of their holidays."

"So why the show? If they aren't any good, let's get rid of them. I think they'd be more suited to the harbor tourist traps than a reputable gallery like this one."

"I didn't say they weren't any good, just not up to your mother's caliber. And she wants to have a showing of some of his work. There are so many other galleries they could choose to represent their work, but she chose this one." And maybe holding the showing would assuage some of her own guilt. Would things have turned out differently if she'd given Jordan a one-man show like he'd asked?

"So you're doing this for my mother?"

"Primarily."

"What happened at his showing last winter?" Jed asked.

"What showing last winter?" she asked. A sinking feeling swamped her, remembering his obsession for a show. Had Jordan turned elsewhere? Maybe another gallery owner had found something in his work she'd missed. She looked at the picture, searching for an elusive aspect that would change its value.

"He said he was going to have a one-man show, said he'd invite me to the gala event. It pays to have connections in the art world, as I recalled the letter went. When no invitation came, I assumed he'd just forgotten. Not that I could have come. I was in Brazil at the time."

"He didn't have a show that I know of," Laura said, remembering how passionately he'd pushed her for the chance. But he'd not wanted an alcove at the gallery when she had halfheartedly suggested that compromise. Jordan had wanted to commandeer the entire showroom in a solo production. Jordan's assessment of his work differed from Laura's.

"You'd know—it was this gallery he was talking about," Jed said.

She turned back to the large table in the center of the room. Jed followed her with his eyes.

Laura was in the middle of a family situation she didn't want to be involved with. She didn't know all the ins and outs, but this man was not the beloved son Jordan had been. Was there going to be a fight about Jordan's estate? Nothing was as it seemed. She wished not for the first time that she'd never met Jordan Brodie. Never fallen in love with the man. Never discovered him in bed with that beautiful woman.

"Jordan wanted to have an exclusive one-man show with no other paintings or sculptures to compete. I couldn't do that. It never went any farther than discussion. I'm sorry if he thought otherwise." She'd known he'd never been happy with her decision. He'd constantly pushed to have her display his work; and she'd constantly refused.

"When were you two going to get married?" Jed asked abruptly.

"We never set a date," she said shortly. "Why?"

"For a grieving almost-wife, you seem fairly resigned to his death," he commented.

"For me it happened three months ago, you're the one who just learned about it," she said. "I don't wish to get in the middle of a family argument. Your mother and father asked me to do this. If, as executor of the estate, you say no, I will go along with your decision. But you need to inform your mother."

Laura tried to think of all the different things she'd have to deal with to stop a show at this stage. The caterer would be all right. She'd have to write off the prepublicity. Maybe she could get the printer to cut her a break. She used him exclusively, so maybe he'd be generous.

Jed turned back to the paintings, pulling the first one forward so he could see the next one, and the next. Soon he'd looked at every one she'd selected.

"This all?"

"All I'm planning to show. I've allocated the alcove to the left for Jordan's work. Your mother isn't pleased with it, but it's the best I can offer."

"He has more?"

"Of course. As far as I know he never sold a thing. He has stacks of canvasses at the cottage. I chose the ones that I thought best represented his work." And had the most chance for a sale in case Maria changed her mind.

"My mother didn't choose these?" Jed asked, replacing them against the wall.

"She can't bring herself to look at them yet. She trusts me to do the best for him." Laura wondered if Maria would continue in that trust if she ever learned Laura had broken the engagement the day before Jordan had died. She looked away, remembering. It would be a long time before she'd forget that betrayal. She'd loved him and he'd thrown that away. But to keep his mother from knowing, Laura had not told anyone. She didn't think the distraught woman could cope with more.

"Has she ever seen his work?" Jed asked.

"I suppose so. Why wouldn't she have seen what he was doing over the years?" Laura had never questioned that. The dinners she'd attended focused on discussion about works in progress. Jordan always had a good story about what he was working on. Had Maria seen his recent paintings?

"My mother recognizes talent. There is very little showing here."

"Maybe as a mother, she thinks everything her sons do is perfect," Laura said, wondering not for the first time what Maria's reaction would be when she saw the work hanging from the gallery walls. To hear her talk, Jordan had extraordinary talent. She was going to be so disappointed. Laura had asked her several times to come look at the paintings. Maria steadfastly refused.

"Not all sons," he said absently. "Can you give me an appraisal for tax purposes? Not just of these, but of all he did?"

Laura nodded slowly. She could do a formal appraisal. She'd done it before and her credentials gave her the expertise to be accepted by the IRS. However, she wasn't sure she wanted to. She was trying to forget Jordan, move on with her life. What would being surrounded by his work, visiting the cottage where she'd been so happy and so devastated, do to her equilibrium?

"I'm heading to his cottage next. How many canvasses will I find there?"

"Lots. I never inventoried or counted. He has them stacked against the walls of his studio."

Jed glanced at his watch. "Have you had lunch yet?"

Surprised at the question she shook her head.

"Come eat with me and tell me what I need to know about art and how it's appraised and how much it'll cost and how long the appraisal process will take," Jed said—ordered more like.

"There're other appraisers around. Maybe you should get one of them." She didn't want to go back to the cottage.

"Conflict of interest?"

"I would give you an honest assessment. But you might wish for someone else." Would she truly give a reliable, unbiased appraisal or would the hurt and anguish of the last few months color her opinions? No, where art was concerned, nothing stood in the way of her honest and forthright opinion.

"You know his work. You'd be best."

Jed's attention focused on her. Those dark eyes seemed to peer deep into her innermost part. Her breath caught for a moment. She felt a warmth and curiosity that surprised her. What was there about this man that caught her unaware? He was grieving for his brother. That should give them a common bond. She grieved for Jordan's death. And for the lost love she'd so happily embraced.

Laura blinked. She could almost feel the energy radiating from Jed. The focus on her was unsettling. He was not at all like Jordan despite his looks. She'd do well not to confuse the two just because they looked identical.

"I'm not really keen on that kind of work," she said, stalling. She didn't want to spend any more time with Jed Brodie than absolutely necessary. Or with the bittersweet memories of Jordan when he first began courting her.

"But you know art values."

She nodded.

"You don't want my folks to know everything is worthless, is that it? They'll blame you if you don't appraise it high? And that would damage your relationship," Jed guessed.

She shook her head. "I never said Jordan's paintings are worthless. They are not up to your mother's work. She thinks he was tremendously talented. I hate to be the one to disappoint her. I like your mother."

"Don't worry about Mom. Where art is concerned, she's totally honest."

Laura was trying to gradually pull back from Maria and Jefferson and their grief. She longed for the business relationship she'd enjoyed when Hugo was still alive and running the gallery. Before Jordan had swept her off her feet. Before things had gone so wrong and emotions and relationships became tangled.

She studied the man in front of her another minute. He looked so much like Jordan she had to keep reminding herself he wasn't. If he kept looking at her, she'd forget business decorum and reach out to touch him. Once burned, twice shy was the old saying. She needed to be more cautious in her personal life from now on. Not take at face value words designed to convince her she was special. This man was yummy to look at, but was he any different from his brother on the inside?

"It's only lunch," he said, amusement creeping into his eyes.

Her bones felt as though they were melting. That look was captivating. She turned away, trying to get control of herself. This was not Jordan. And if he were, she'd be furious with him.

"Come and fill me in. We can visit the cottage afterward and you can give me an estimate on time and cost for an appraisal."

His tone was almost cajoling. Maybe he also had some of that charm that Jordan displayed.

She needed to think this through. On the one hand, it was merely business. She could assess the paintings, do a written report and add some much needed funds to the coffers. She could handle that.

On the other hand, the man was a constant, vivid reminder of Jordan. Her emotions were still in turmoil. Could she forget the past and do the work without some emotional cost? And without becoming infatuated with the spitting image of the man she'd loved until three months ago?

She turned toward the door. "I need to get my purse and let Heather know I'll be gone for lunch. But I can't go to the cottage this afternoon, I have an appointment at two." She would take this one step at a time. If she could manage lunch with Jed, it would give her an idea of how working with him might be.

"So we'll discuss when you can schedule the appraisal over lunch. Get your purse, I want to look at the rest of these paintings." He turned his attention back to the canvasses stacked in the rack.

Laura had a feeling she was making a mistake. She still held the envelope he'd given her. Maybe she could quickly read through the papers to make sure Jed was who he said he was. She couldn't imagine agreeing to his demands and finding out later it was all false.

As she walked through the display area to return to her office, she was pleased to notice several people browsing. Heather stood by attentively, yet let them gaze at whatever they wanted without interrupting them. The gallery was located right on Harbor Street, the main thoroughfare of Miragansett. The colorful historic town was a tourist mecca in the summer months. Hugo had opened the gallery decades ago, before the current interest in old getaways swept the monied set. It was the best location in town.

Once inside her office, Laura opened the envelope. Inside

was a copy of Jordan's will. She had not been at the reading as he had left her nothing having written the will long before he met her. She'd been surprised a man that young even had a will. It was short and to the point—he requested his estate be liquidated and the money divided between his parents and his brother, except for *whatever paintings of mine my brother Jed wants.* He'd appointed Jed as executor.

"Probably because he's the only one in the family who isn't the artistic type," she murmured.

The letter from the attorney outlined his duties and authority. Jed Brodie was the man to deal with, not Maria or Jefferson. And even if they wished to keep the paintings, they couldn't. They'd have to purchase them from the estate. How ironic.

Laura reached into the drawer for her purse wondering how this would complicate her life. Nothing was ever the way it seemed when dealing with the Brodies.

CHAPTER TWO

JED stood near one of the large plate-glass windows at the front of the gallery gazing out over the busy street when Laura finally left her office. He felt like he was in some kind of time warp. His parents had not been overjoyed to see him. His mother accused him of deliberately staying away from the funeral. He'd explained about the timing of the message, but she refused to accept any responsibility on its delay, saying she'd told the woman who answered to have him call. It was more trouble than it was worth to keep repeating she should have mentioned it was a family emergency.

Sometimes he wondered how his mother made it in the real world. She expected everything to run according to her rules and when they didn't, it was never her fault.

Being an artist was the cause. She lived that mystique for all it was worth. Jed remembered making meals when he was in high school so the entire family could eat. His mother would be lost in oil paints, his father in his studio working. Jordan had either been out with some girl or talking on the phone.

How did they manage meals now, he wondered briefly.

"I'm ready," Laura said, coming to stand next to him.

He glanced at the woman his brother had been going to marry. He didn't understand this relationship, either. Laura was not the type of woman he knew Jordan liked. She didn't have big blond hair, wasn't built like a Playboy bunny and seemed all-around stable. Her honey-golden hair barely brushed her shoulders. Her brown eyes held honest appraisal when she looked at him. She wore little makeup. Her dress was suitable for a successful businesswoman. Had his brother finally given up his bimbos and settled down with someone who could add stability to his life?

Or had he proposed to insure he always had a market for his painting? The cynical thought wasn't fair to Laura. She was a pretty woman, as well as being a competent business owner. The gallery was obviously doing well. Maybe his brother had finally matured and had been ready to settle down. Jed had not seen him for the last five years. A man could change in that time. Maybe love was the key factor here. He'd heard love could change the world.

"Where do you recommend we eat?" he asked.

"Sal's Shack has good seafood sandwiches. It's crowded but there's always a table somewhere," she said. "Unless you have another place in mind?"

"No. I don't know the area. My folks moved here when I was in college. I've been here for only a few visits since then."

Jed opened the large glass door for her and followed her into the sunshine. The wide sidewalks were not crowded despite the number of people strolling along. It was late June, the beginning of the summer months when tourists outnumbered the residence five to one. The summer economy kept the town going year-round, but the other visits he'd made had been in fall. He thought he liked the place better when it wasn't so crowded.

He looked at her. "Didn't Jordan tell you?"

She kept her gaze forward and shook her head quickly. "I knew your family was a fairly recent transplant as Miragansett families go. But they were here before me, so they seemed like longtime residents to me. Jordan wasn't much for talking about the past. He was always looking toward the future and what success he'd achieve when his painting took off."

Or he'd make love talk. The hours they spent together were for the two of them, not talking about his family or the past.

"He was thirty years old, how long before his painting took off?" Jed asked.

Laura shrugged. She slipped dark glasses over her eyes. She didn't want to talk about Jordan.

Jed tried not to let it bother him that his brother had not shared more information about their family with Laura, but he wondered what kind of engagement it had been. How could she agree to marry him and not know more about the Brodies?

"How long were you two engaged?" he asked.

"We were engaged for two months," she said.

"And you knew him how long before that?"

She glanced up at him, her expression hard to read with the dark glasses. "Is that important?"

"Just curious."

"Jordan swept me off my feet and we got engaged only a couple of months after meeting. I'd known your mother for longer, of course. Hugo represented some of her work so I knew her first from business."

"So how did you two meet?" He wasn't surprised to hear Jordan had swept her off her feet. He had that ability. Jed knew he'd never sweep anyone off their feet. He didn't have the glib charm that Jordan displayed so easily. For him life was more serious. He didn't think the world owed him anything. He had to make his own way. A slight, but significant difference between the two of them.

Women liked the carefree charm of his brother, Jed knew. There'd been plenty of instances when they'd been in school and college. He was nothing like Jordan in that area. The few women he'd dated over the last decade had been casual friends. His work in foreign countries didn't make for long-term relationships.

"He came into the shop about a year and a half after I became the owner. He brought a painting to show me, wanting me to represent him. I declined based on the one painting, but he was persistent, insisted on taking me to dinner to discuss things. We began dating and before long he asked me to marry him. I said yes."

Where was the falling-in-love part? Jed wondered. Maybe Laura was still too raw from Jordan's death to talk about that. Yet there was a hint of anger in her tone. Wasn't that part of the grieving process, anger that the person who died had left?

"You two were obviously not very close," she commented.

"Distances prevented it." Distance and their past. Jed kept secrets few people knew he had. Jordan had moved on, why couldn't he?

"With today's e-mail and telephones everywhere, you could have kept in closer contact if you both had wanted. I always thought twins were close," she said.

"Maybe ones who share more than just looks. I don't have the family artist talent. Jordan couldn't care less about load ratios and wind factors. He went his way and I went mine."

"And never the two shall meet," she finished. "I didn't even know you were twins," she said sadly.

Jed looked at her in surprise. "Jordan didn't speak of me at all?"

"Only to say you were the younger brother and worked out of the country and the family rarely saw you. Which explained why you weren't at home for Christmas."

Jed didn't want it to bother him, but it did. How could his brother be so close to this woman and not even mention they were twins? He had never fully understood Jordan. This was another incident to add to the list.

They reached Sal's Shack. It was situated right on the harbor, with a huge wooden deck jutting over the water, dotted with umbrellas to shade the tables—most of which were full of laughing, happy tourists and townsfolk eating lunch. The hostess led them to one of the umbrella-shaded spots near the railing. The bay was calm today, ruffled only occasionally by a gust of wind. The blue was deeper than that of the clear sky. A perfect June afternoon in Miragansett.

Jed saw one or two people look their way as they walked through the crowd and do a double-take. They probably had known Jordan. Were they others who had not known he had a twin?

He felt overdressed. Everyone on the deck was in casual shorts and cropped shirts. Dark glasses repelled the sun's glare. Some had hats that lifted slightly in the gust of breeze from the sea. His suit was as out of place here as at the bridge site.

As soon as he returned to his hotel, he'd change into something more casual. It'd been a long time since he'd taken a vacation. He'd planned to combine the business of Jordan's estate with some time relaxing in the seaside town. Working in the jungle he wore khakis and the coolest cotton he could. Those clothes would fit in here, as well, he thought, surveying the other men.

He looked at Laura. Her dress was pale pink and looked cool, sort of casual, yet businesslike. Her hair blew away from her face which left it available to his gaze. Her skin was lightly tanned, her dark glasses hiding her eyes from his.

He wondered what she thought about dealing with him now, instead of his mother.

He'd already run into trouble with his mom on the terms of Jordan's will. She didn't approve of Jed's having the control and claimed she should have all of Jordan's paintings. It was a formality only; if she had to she could buy them all. The money went into the estate and then it would be divided back between him and his parents. Still, he planned to follow the letter of the will. Jordan had obviously written it for a reason.

Jed had been surprised to get a call from the lawyer once he'd spoken to his mother. He had not known Jordan had named him as executor. Everything had been put on hold until Jed could be located.

He and Laura both ordered the shrimp subsandwiches and iced tea. The hum of many conversations gave a background white noise. Above it, the slap of waves on the sand beneath the deck could barely be heard. The erratic breeze from the sea kept the temperature manageable, though Jed did slip off the suit jacket and roll back his shirtsleeves.

"It's hot. Not many men wear suits here," she commented.

"I came straight from the airport. I saw my parents briefly then came to see you," he explained. Now he wished he'd changed first. Still, he was on a short time frame and was impatient to get things going. He felt like a fish out of water here. He wanted to wind up the estate and get back to work. His second in command could handle things, but Jed liked to run the construction site himself.

"I read the will," she said. "It appears you have full authority. How does that impact the show? Will you let it proceed?" She withdrew the envelope from her purse and handed it back to him.

"I knew nothing about the proposed show. When I discussed it with the lawyer who wrote the will, we made plans to liquidate assets as soon as possible. We're already three months after his death. My mother can buy his pictures, based on your appraisals, and show them if she wishes. If his paintings weren't selling, what was he doing for money?"

Laura didn't know how much their family talked to each other. Not much if Jed's questions were anything to go by. She was curious about the true relationship. Jordan had said so little about his brother, or anything else actually—except how fabulously they'd live once his paintings sold. And how much he loved her. How he would treat her like a queen when the money began to roll in.

Foolish pipe dreams she now knew better than to believe. Her face flushed in memories of the love they'd shared. How she never asked questions, always content to bask in the moment. She'd been an idiot in retrospect. But what a blissful few weeks she'd had.

Jed was watching her. What had he asked?

"Your mother subsidized him until he began to sell." She tried to keep her tone neutral. Her parents lived a modest life-style in Iowa. She'd been raised to become self-sufficient at a young age. She couldn't imagine her own parents thinking they had to support her at this point in her life. She looked away. That was unfair. They would have helped her in a moment's notice if she'd really needed it. Maria had lots of money; she probably didn't think two thoughts about subsidizing Jordan.

"He was thirty and hadn't begun to earn a living. Would he really ever have?" Jed asked.

She bit her lip, feeling the wash of guilt. Would it have hurt her any to have hung one or two of his paintings in her gallery? Maybe some tourist would have bought them and given Jordan a boost that could have changed his future.

"It's hard to say." Because she had not given him that chance.

She looked at Jed, feeling surreal talking to the man who looked so like Jordan. His features were identical. Only the shorter haircut and different attitude showed her she wasn't living in some dream or caught up in the past. She could be excused for the awareness that hovered. He looked like someone she loved. Her body had a hard time differentiating between them. But her mind knew. She wasn't going down that idyllic path a second time.

Their sandwiches came and for a moment conversation was suspended while they began to eat.

"Tell me about yourself," Jed said a little later. "You're not from here...I can tell from your accent."

She laughed and put down the sandwich she was about to take another bite from. "I like to think I have no accent and those from here are the ones with the definite accent. I'm from Iowa. I went to college in Boston, studied fine arts, then looked for the ideal job. I found a less than ideal one in Boston where I had the opportunity to learn all I could about current art, appraising, marketing. I spent weekends and vacations looking for another position. A few years ago I came to Miragansett for a long weekend, fell in love with the place and began to look for a job. Hugo Atkins was kind enough to hire me and here I've been ever since."

"It's a nice town, what little I've seen over the years. My parents lived in Boston until I started college. I've been on my own since, and for the most part on assignments out of the country, so I've never spent much time here. But I remember my mother raving about Hugo's gallery. It was one of the best in all of Cape Cod, she once said."

"I like to think it still is. He died almost two years ago. I was fortunate he left the business to me," she said quietly.

He raised an eyebrow at that but before he could speak, he heard a rise in the conversation level. Turning, he saw his mother. Maria Brodie wove her way through the tables until she stopped at theirs.

"What are you doing talking to Laura?" she demanded, frowning at her son.

Jed rose politely. "I didn't expect you to join us for lunch," he said easily.

"I'm not joining you!"

She glared at Laura. "I called the gallery. Heather told me you had come here to have lunch with Jed. He's nothing like Jordan. He's only here to wreak havoc with our lives."

Jed was glad to see some things never changed—like his mother's bent for dramatics.

Turning back to her son, she continued, "Haven't we had enough heartache with Jordan's death without your interfering with our plans?" Her dramatic tone seemed to expand to include the entire deck and all the people there. Most of the customers at nearby tables stopped eating, fascinated by the scene unfolding.

"I'm only following Jordan's instructions, Mother. You saw the will, you know this is what he wanted," Jed said quietly. He knew better than to try to head her off. She loved an audience. Did she realize so many people were watching?

"He wrote that several years ago. Things have changed. He should have left me the paintings, or at least left them to Laura. She was going to be his wife. It's not fair!"

Laura started to open her mouth, thought better of it and closed it firmly. Glancing around, she saw other diners avidly observing every nuance.

"Maria, please, sit down and join us," she urged. "People are staring."

Maria paused, glanced around haughtily and then sat in the chair Jed quickly drew out for her.

She glowered at her son. "You stay away from Jordan's fiancée. I remember the rivalry you two boys had, always trying to take away each other's girls. You can't have Laura. He was happy here, away from your interference. Stay away from Laura!"

"Then shall I find someone else to appraise Jordan's paintings? We were having lunch to discuss that," Jed said easily, sitting back in his chair. He wondered if he was going to be able to finish his sandwich. How did his mother live with such high drama all the time? He'd find it wearing.

Maria looked surprised. She glanced at Laura. "Of course I want Laura to appraise his work. She'd do a marvelous job. She loved Jordan and admired his paintings, right dear?"

Laura gave a polite smile but kept quiet, lest she end the months of silence and tell Maria exactly what she'd thought of Jordan, and how she'd ended their engagement twenty-four hours before he crashed his car against that tree. If and when she told, it would not be at a crowded restaurant with potential customers listening avidly.

Actually, she had no plans to bring more heartbreak to Maria. The woman had loved the idea of their marriage. She had been needy after her son's death, relying on Laura for several things since then. Her heart ached as Maria's must. She didn't want to cause any problems for the family.

"I would appraise the paintings to the best of my ability," she said.

"There!" Maria looked in triumph to Jed. "She's the best for the job."

Jed inclined his head slightly, a smile tugging at his lips. "So glad you approve my choice."

Laura admired his patience. She drew a deep breath, determined not to get upset with Maria this afternoon. She'd had enough turmoil already this day.

"She's one of the best art dealers in town," Maria said. She looked at what they were eating. "I'll have the shrimp, also," she said.

Jed summoned the waitress and placed an order for his mother.

Maria ignored Jed and looked at Laura. "I planned to stop by the gallery to look at that alcove again. I think it's too small and not light enough for the best display of his paintings."

"Mother," Jed interrupted. "Have you seen the pictures Laura picked out for the show?"

"Not yet." Maria paused a moment, then took a deep breath. "I cannot bring myself to see my darling boy's work. I know I will be devastated all over again. It's all I can do to make it through each day. Planning this retrospective has given me something to focus on. I'm sure opening night will be almost more than I can bear."

For a moment Laura thought Maria might start crying. She'd been inconsolable at the funeral. Laura had visited a few times since, spacing the visits longer and longer apart. One day they would move back into the realm of gallery owner-artist, but for the time being, she was destined to play the part of grieving fiancée. Half the time she felt like such a fraud. The other half, she genuinely grieved and wished fervently that

Jordan Brodie was still alive and she'd never walked in on him that afternoon.

"They are not up to your standards," Jed said.

Maria waved her hands in the air as if that was of no importance. "Probably not yet. I've had twenty years more experience than he had. But the talent was there. Given time, he probably would have been one of the leading painters of the twenty-first century."

Laura blinked. Maria was really living in a fantasy world. "No," she said involuntarily.

Maria and Jed looked at her.

"What?"

Laura shifted position slightly, glancing at Jed in appeal. "The paintings are nothing like what you do, Maria. I don't believe Jordan had the discipline you have to continue to grow in his work." She stopped short. If what Jed said earlier was true, Maria needed to see the paintings to know her precious son would never have achieved her level of success.

Unless he stopped drinking, of course. Maybe his entire life would have been different had he not wanted to party more than anything. Why hadn't she realized that at the time? She'd enjoyed their clubbing as much as he had. But she would not have continued forever. Would he ever have settled in marriage? She'd never know.

"Come by the gallery and see them," Laura continued. "Help me choose which frames to use for the different subjects I've chosen. If you don't like them, we have time to select others from his inventory."

"Oh, I couldn't bear it. I don't know how I shall be able to be at the showing, yet for my poor son, I shall be there. But I don't believe I can see them more than once so soon after his death."

"You need to view them before the show," Jed said. "They aren't very good."

"How dare you besmirch your brother's work! From the

time he was seven or eight years old, he showed great promise. We all know you have no artistic talent, Jed. Don't belittle what you can't do yourself!"

Jed's eyes narrowed as if in anger. But his voice remained calm when he spoke, "I can't draw worth a damn, but I do recognize raw talent, and it's not there."

The waitress arrived with Maria's sandwich.

"Wrap it up, I'm leaving," she said imperiously. She rose. Jed rose. Laura watched bemused as they stared at each other for a long moment. Maria spoke again,

"I expect the show to proceed as planned. I trust Laura to have selected the best of his work and once the community sees the paintings, everyone will realize the loss to the art world his death caused. You're the executor, figure out how to have those paintings be available for the show." She followed the waitress back toward the restaurant proper to get her wrapped sandwich.

Jed sat and looked at Laura.

"She's heading for a big disappointment."

"The paintings aren't that bad," Laura said diplomatically.

"They aren't that good. She expects to see masterpieces. Instead she's going to see mediocre work. Are those the best?"

Laura nodded, fiddling with her iced tea glass.

"He liked to have a good time, didn't want to be responsible, accountable, or grow up. And there was no need, as long as Mom subsidized him," Jed said with frustration.

Laura said nothing. She began to eat again, but the sandwich tasted like cardboard. As soon as she could, without looking as if she were fleeing, she wanted to leave.

"So when can you come out to do the appraisal?" he asked.

He was relentless. "Not before Thursday afternoon," she said. Today was Tuesday; if he was in such a rush, maybe he'd not want to wait that long. She began to think it would suit her better to have another appraiser handle the task. She felt battered from all the drama of the day.

"Fine. What time?"

"Two?" Drat. She should have said she was busy until next week, or next month. Or just flat out told him no. She glanced at him. She didn't think many people told him no.

"I'll be there. I have to clear out Jordan's things. See if there is anything else worth selling. Most of his clothes I'll donate. Do you have a recommendation where?"

"There's a thrift store in Provincetown that supports a children's group. If I were doing it, I would donate there."

"What of his things do you want?" he asked gently.

Laura shook her head. "There is not one thing I can think of I want." She was not truly entitled to anything, even if Jed thought differently. She had ended their relationship. Had her ending the engagement caused Jordan to crash his car? She hoped not, but the nagging doubt remained.

She tossed her napkin on the table and rose. "I have to get back to the gallery. Thank you for lunch. I'll see you Thursday." Unless an excuse presented itself before then so she could get out of doing the appraisals without questions being raised.

Jed rose with her and waited until she walked away before sitting down again.

Just as Laura was about to step away from the deck, she glanced back. He sat gazing out over the harbor. For a moment, she thought she caught a glimpse of loneliness. She hesitated. Maybe she'd misjudged Jed Brodie. There was no denying the tug of her heart as she debated returning to the table. For what? To see if she could cheer him up? Nothing could do that. And any close association could lead to a revelation she didn't want made.

Turning, she headed back to the gallery, planning her next appointment. And then she'd turn her attention to appraising the paintings that were currently awaiting framing.

She'd call in Jasper Mullins, as well. He owed her a favor and could give a second opinion. Not that she questioned her judgment. Hugo's instructions over the years and her own experience since gave her confidence in her decisions. But for what she owed Jordan and his parents, she'd see if she could get another opinion.

Jed stayed at the table long enough to finish his meal. He hadn't eaten regularly in the last couple of days with the time zone changes and three different flights. He was hungry and tired. And not looking forward to winding up his brother's affairs. He wished things had been different. He loved his mother. He didn't always understand her, but he knew what she considered important. It had never been about him, always about Jordan. He'd come to terms with that situation years ago.

His father was also in a dream world most of the time, sculpting from marble or granite—revealing what the rock hid, he said. He only surfaced when it was time to sell the piece. He drove a shrewd deal and his pieces were now sought after, by private collectors, as well as modern museums.

The clean salt air felt refreshing after the constant scent of rotting vegetation that permeated the area around the Amazon River basin. He had become used to the smell over the months, only now realizing how foul the air seemed in comparison.

Tossing some money on the table, holding his suit jacket with one finger, he slung it across his shoulder and headed back to his hotel. He'd call the office, let them know he was extending his visit. This was not something he could handle in a day or two.

To appease his mother, he'd let the showing take place. How that would affect probate, he'd have to find out from the attorney. Once he'd unpacked and changed into cooler clothes, he'd head for the cottage and assess what needed to be done there. He couldn't believe he'd never see his brother again. That he wasn't going to be called upon to bail him out of yet another scrape. Or hear some convoluted plan on how Jordan would make a million dollars.

They hadn't been close, but he missed him like hell.

What had his life been like here? Jed had never visited Jordan's cottage. Would the place remind him of Jordan? Or would it be so unknown to him no reminders would arise? He hoped for the latter. He wished Jordan had written his will differently. Jed wished he could still be in the Amazon Basin sweating over delivery of the next supply ship, haranguing the local laborers to work faster or the blasted bridge would never be complete. Wouldn't that have antagonized his mother, to not even come home once he had learned of Jordan's death?

Yet there was nothing to be done. Jordan was gone. It was hard to grasp he'd never see his brother again. Never find that magic moment when they'd be close as they had been as young boys, before the obvious favoritism of their parents had caused the schism. Death was very final.

CHAPTER THREE

LAURA sat on the sole lounge chair on her minuscule balcony, gazing at the narrow wedge of the sea visible from her third floor flat. The evening was pleasant. She'd put on a baggy T-shirt to sleep in, brought out a glass of white wine and propped her feet on the railing. No one could see her as she sat in the darkness. It was one of her favorite times of the day. As the ocean breeze cooled the night air, she let her thoughts drift. Time and again they returned to Jed Brodie and the ambivalent feelings she had around him. She didn't like him. He reminded her of what she wanted to forget. Yet she felt sadness for his loss. Despite his relationship with his brother, it had to hurt when a sibling died. Laura was an only child, but she could use her imagination.

She knew better than to give into her softer side. Jed wasn't Jordan. A man less needful of someone fussing over him she hadn't met. She'd fallen for Jordan fast and lived to regret it. Could she trust her judgment about men? Especially Brodie men?

Yet she was not one to sugarcoat things. She'd been attracted to him. His tanned features looked rugged and masculine. The way he'd looked at her with those dark eyes, as if she was the only thing to focus on, she had one hundred percent of his attention when he looked at her. She shivered in memory.

Her phone rang. She went inside and got her portable, returning to the balcony as she clicked it on.

"This is Laura," she said, settling down again.

"Is it too late to call?"

She recognized Jed's voice instantly. Suddenly she was fully alert, on edge. Why was he calling?

"Not at all. What can I do for you?"

The darkness hid all things. She could talk to him and keep her secrets.

There was a moment of silence on the other end.

"Jed?"

"This is probably a bad idea," he said.

"What is?"

"Calling to ask you about Jordan. You probably have a million things to do."

"Actually I'm sitting on my balcony enjoying the night air. Where are you?"

"In a hotel room without a view. One of the last ones left and lucky to get that, according to the desk clerk. The television has nothing on it to warrant my attention. After eighteen months in Brazil, you'd think I'd have plenty to catch up on. I don't know anyone in town except my parents and you. And I guess that's a tenuous connection at best."

"What can I tell you?"

"How he was these last few months. What he was interested in. Besides you, of course. Was he happy?"

She took a sip of her wine, stalling. She didn't want to remember the last few months. "I think Jordan had the capability of being happy no matter what. He never seemed to take anything seriously enough to impact his outlook on life. It was one of the things about him that appealed to me. I worry about the gallery, worry about keeping a steady flow of quality artwork coming in and selling. Worry about taxes and the weather and lots of things. Jordan never did. And when I was with him, I'd forget and have fun."

It was what she missed most about him, she realized.

"Yeah, he had an optimistic outlook that didn't quit," Jed said slowly.

"He used to make me mad sometimes, never thinking the worst would come. But he was so often right, the worst didn't happen. He had a lot of friends, none close that I know of, but plenty to hang out with, go clubbing, or sailing. He loved being around people—which surprised me a little," she said slowly. She was again coming to realize some things that should have given her clues to the real Jordan.

"Why's that?"

"Most of the artists I know are content to be their own best friend. Jordan had scads of friends. He was not a loner."

"We were different in that aspect. Actually we were different in many ways, not just that. He always seemed to have a flair for making friends. From the time we were in elementary school together, he had a circle of friends for any occasion."

"Did you?"

"I had a few friends. Hung on the outskirts of his groups if I didn't have anyone to hang out with. He was generous that way."

"He was freehanded. I wish…" Laura trailed off.

"What?"

"That I had appreciated how he was before he died. I think I wanted him to change, and of course no one can change once they are a certain age—unless they wish it. I loved his carefree attitude, but wanted him to be more practical. I loved going to parties with him, yet yearned for quiet evenings at home. What does that say about me?"

"That you wanted a balanced life, not all one-sided."

"You make that sound nicer than I think it was." Not that any of it mattered once she'd discovered him in bed with that woman. She closed her eyes, wishing she had another memory to supplant that one. It was the worst one she could remember him by.

"You're at the hotel?" she said a minute later. "Why aren't

you staying at your parents' house? Or staying at the cottage? Your mother rents that cottage, you could stay there."

"Let's just say it's easier to come and go if there are no family dynamics to get in the way."

Laura frowned. What did that mean? "Did you get a lot done today?"

Again there was a pause. Laura could hear rustling in the background. Suddenly she wondered if he had gotten ready for bed as she had. Was he in boxers, or nothing at all? Jordan had slept in the nude, did his brother?

Her heart raced as her thoughts veered away from the conversation. Dragging them back, she chastised herself for the wayward ideas. Jed was Jordan's brother!

"I went through his clothes, packed them all in bags. There weren't as many ghosts as I expected," Jed said.

"Ghosts?"

"Memories. We were inseparable as boys. We began to go our separate ways in high school and, after our first year in college acknowledged we were too far apart in our philosophies of life to keep in close touch. I bet I only saw Jordan a half dozen times in the last decade."

"Your choice, or his?" she asked. Jordan had not seemed to miss his brother. Had that been only a facade? There was so much she didn't know about the man she'd once thought she'd marry. Another clue they weren't suited. Why hadn't she picked up on them at the time?

"Mutual." He was silent. "Actually more on my part than his. I was tired of—" He stopped abruptly.

"Tired of what?" she asked.

"Cleaning up after him. It's not important. Water long over the dam now."

"It's hard to hold on to anger when the person is gone, isn't it?" she said slowly. "He was wonderful at first, then changed a little. Now I'd give anything to have him back—warts and all."

Could she have forgiven him as he'd begged? Once trust was shattered, she didn't know how to rebuild it.

"Some things seem insignificant after all," Jed said. He took a breath she could hear over the line.

"Changing the subject, what did you do this afternoon?"

"Instead of coming to the cottage, do you mean?"

"You had plans when I showed up. I was merely curious as to what."

"I met with a client who loves to collect certain glass sculpture. She and I have been working together from the time I first joined Hugo. She's a lovely elderly lady who has enough money to indulge herself."

"Sell her anything?"

"Not today. I had nothing I thought suitable for her. But we had a lovely tea and I promised to keep my eye out for just what she wants."

"That all?"

"There's more to running an art gallery than sitting around and waiting for people to wander in and buy," she said. Did he think she didn't work hard at her job?

"I didn't mean that. As I said, just curious. Sometime you'll have to tell me all that's involved in running a successful art gallery."

"Maybe I will."

"Jordan's place was dusty. Did he have a maid or something? I can't see my brother cleaning a house. Or am I wrong?"

She smiled, feeling the ache fade. "Actually I can't see Jordan cleaning house, either. Planning for a blowout party, yes. He had a cleaning service once a week. Maybe your mother suspended the service after his death. I know she hasn't been to the cottage since he died. She's grieving so it hurts to see her so sad."

"I know. It's going to take her a long time to get over this, if she ever does."

Laura wondered if it would take Jed a long time to get over his twin's death. She wished she knew him well enough to ask.

"Do you want me to bring you your things from there? Or will you pick them up on Thursday?" he asked.

Laura felt as if she'd been slapped. She knew nothing of hers remained at Jordan's. "There's nothing I want," she said slowly.

"Nothing?"

She didn't recognize the odd tone to his voice. Should she have taken whatever was there and not raised questions?

How to explain she'd cleared out everything she'd had there the afternoon she'd walked in on Jordan and that young woman in his bed. Any feminine apparel had to belong to the other woman.

What a tired cliché. The hurt and betrayal rose again. She was so angry with Jordan she could slap him, if he were still here. How could he lie to her so?

"I want nothing—donate everything. Maybe I should have sorted through the clothing," she said. She would have found anger a driving force to get everything packed up and donated. Anger at herself for being so gullible and falling for a glib charmer. And anger at Jordan for using her and not being honest. Anger that he'd been seeing someone else while professing he loved her. Anger at shattering the dreams she'd built of their future.

Anger that she had not proved to be what he needed as she'd once thought he was what she needed.

"It wasn't that hard. I packed up the clothes out of the closet and drawers. The clothes still in the dirty hamper I just tossed. The rest I figured were clean. Maybe you can give me the address of the thrift shop and I'll drop them there tomorrow."

Quickly she ran through the things she needed to do the next day. Guilt made her volunteer, "I could go over with you if you want. It's not hard to find if you know Provincetown, but a bit tricky to give directions as I don't know the street names, just how to find the place."

"I thought you were busy until Thursday afternoon," he said.

"I said that's when I could start the appraisals. The process takes time and concentration. I have a bit of free time tomorrow afternoon, take it or leave it." She already regretted her hasty comments. Let Jed find his own thrift shop to donate to.

"I'll take it. I'll take you to dinner afterward in appreciation for your help."

"No need." She didn't like the fluttering that sprang up at the invitation. This was not some man she could become interested in.

"Take pity on a guy alone in town."

That sparked a laugh. "You are the last man I'd take pity on. Stand on the street corner and six beautiful women will line up to go out with you. I know—Jordan had that effect on women." She tried hard to keep the bitterness from her voice. She'd been so happy to think he'd chosen her. What a fool she'd been.

"He always did. But you're wrong. I don't have the same effect."

That she did not believe.

"Tell me about your work. How did you get into building bridges instead of painting seascapes?" She deliberately changed the subject. If he was lonely and wanting to talk, let him talk. He didn't seem comfortable around his parents. With his brother's recent death, he had to be feeling a need to connect.

"Twins can look alike externally, but inside our personalities are unique. I like building things."

"Did you ever try to paint?"

"Oh, I tried the whole nine yards, painting, sculpting, music. My parents were determined to find some artistic talent in both their sons. But I gave up after a while and concentrated on what I wanted to do. I didn't have the talent Jordan showed as a kid," Jed said.

"Having talent and developing it are two different things."

"Most artists have a fire inside to do what they do, whether painting, sculpting, writing. I know my folks do. Jordan didn't. I knew him all his life. He didn't have that passion that other artists have. Did that bother you? As a prospective wife, I mean."

Not at first. In the beginning she'd been so in love, so wrapped up in *them,* she hadn't given his work much notice. It was only after a couple of months, right toward the end—

"Jordan thought he only had to have people see his work and he'd be set for life. It was part of that optimism he had. I'm more concrete in what I need. So we were yin and yang." Would it have grown to be a barrier had he not betrayed her so cruelly?

"So why didn't you give him a show?"

Laura was silent for a long time. "It's very selfish," she said at last, hating to admit the truth. But something about the darkness, about Jed's voice over the telephone line, made it easier to face facts.

"How so?"

"I guard the reputation of the gallery fiercely. He wanted a complete closure of everything but his work. I offered the alcove I'm using now. It wasn't good enough for him. He wanted the entire gallery. I couldn't risk it. My pessimism, I guess. Now I wish I'd pushed harder for a compromise. I so wish he could be at the show, have people buy his paintings." Guilt played a big part. If she'd done more, would he have turned to the other woman?

"You probably think I'm a terrible person to put business before Jordan's wishes."

"Not at all. You have to run your business, not give handouts to anyone who comes along."

She felt as if a weight had lifted. At least someone knew the truth, and didn't condemn her for it. Would he feel the same if she told him the entire story? She doubted it. She had a feeling from what Jed had said and done in the short time she'd known him that he was high on loyalty and commitment. And Jordan had been his twin.

"So I'm to go ahead with the show?" Laura asked.

"Go for it. My parents and I will sort out the legal issues. It means a lot to my mother to see her son's work represented."

"You surprise me."

"Why?"

"Somehow, I think if my parents treated me as yours do you, I wouldn't be as magnanimous." She shouldn't be saying such things, yet somehow she knew concealed in the darkness, things could be said that wouldn't be in the light of day.

"They are my parents," he said simply.

And you love them, she echoed silently. Wasn't it macho to admit to such a thing? It sure didn't fit her image of Jed Brodie. A tough man in a hard business, he'd surprised her with his dealings with his mother at lunch. She'd expected him to blast the woman for her rudeness. He'd evidenced a lot more patience than she'd expected.

"Tell me how you got into building bridges. Why bridges? Where exactly is this bridge you're building? What's it like there?" She wanted to know more about this mysterious twin.

"The Amazon Basin is certainly different from here. For starters, it's humid and muggy 24/7, with rain as regular as the dawn—only at three every afternoon."

Laura settled in to listen to him describe a world so foreign to hers she was intrigued Jed could so easily travel from one to the other. Time seemed to fly by as he talked about the primitive locale, the untrained locals working with the skilled men from his company. When he talked about some of the snafus they'd experienced, she laughed. She knew it was hard work, but he had a way of making it sound entertaining.

Her distrust gradually eased. He was a man needed for a difficult task. She could let go some of her dislike. He wasn't his brother. She needed to remember that. Nothing would bring Jordan back or give them a second chance. That had passed.

She had a new future to forge. But it wouldn't hurt to talk to Jed a little longer.

It was after eleven when Jed said, "I've bored you enough."

"Not at all. You have a way with words. I felt I was right there. I bet you can't wait to get back."

"I like my work, but I don't miss the constant heat and insects. Being in Miragansett is a refreshing change. Short though the break is."

"How long are you staying?"

"Depends on how long all this takes. I'll pick you up at the gallery tomorrow afternoon so you can show me the way to the thrift shop."

"Around four should give us time enough to get there. They close at five."

"Good night, Laura, thanks for listening."

"Thank you, Jed, for the travelogue."

Jed hung up the receiver. He'd been gazing out the window as they'd talked, seeing the lights from a portion of the town, wishing his room had a view of the bay. If he stayed long enough, he'd ask to change when one of those rooms became available.

His room was dark. He had to get some sleep. It had been interesting talking with Laura. He'd felt closer to Jordan when she spoke of their time together. From the sound of things, Jordan had been the same right up to his death. He'd always drawn the women like flies. Flirting with them, he still had the knack of making each one feel uniquely special. Had he settled down with Laura?

The most interesting aspect of the entire conversation, however, was the fact she didn't want the women's clothing he'd found at the cottage. She'd sounded odd when he brought it up. Were they not hers? If not, then whose? From a long-ago girlfriend? Or a not-so-long ago girlfriend?

Or had Jordan been cheating on the side?

The thought made him sick. Laura was too nice to have his brother treat her so badly. Jed would never forget the trouble Jordan got them into at college. Had he continued his predilection for a variety of women even after he'd asked Laura to marry him? Jed scowled in disgust. It would be just like Jordan—thinking he was free to do whatever until the marriage vows were exchanged. Or even beyond?

When he thought about it, Jed was constantly amazed that two boys from the same parents, same upbringing, could turn out to view life so differently.

He'd left the feminine apparel out on the bed in Jordan's cottage, thinking it had to belong to Laura, thought the sexy black barely there underwear didn't seem to fit her image. But business attire could differ drastically from intimate apparel. First thing in the morning, he'd bag those clothes and hope the thrift shop just took the bags without opening to inventory the contents.

Rising, he walked to the open window. The fresh salt breeze blew cool air into the room. The humid, rotten-vegetation air of the jungle was almost forgotten. It had been a long time since he'd taken much time off from work. He had weeks and weeks of vacation accrued on the books. He'd thought he'd make this trip in a few days, but now wondered if he should stay and see the showing for his brother's paintings. It would most likely be the only showing given. He knew Laura was doing it for sentimental reasons and to placate his mother. He'd suspected that from the moment he'd seen Jordan's work.

It wouldn't hurt her business. Most people understood sentimentality, even if they didn't subscribe to it. To dedicate an alcove to honor her dead fiancé's memory was a fine tribute.

He leaned against the window frame and continued to gaze out over the few lights in the city he could see, but his mind was focused on Laura Parkerson. He and Jordan had never shared the same taste in woman. Before. But this time, he could definitely be interested in the pretty gallery owner. Except—even if she ever returned his regard, how would he know it was him she was thinking of and not Jordan? A ghost was a powerful thing to compete with—especially one that looked exactly like him. There was no room in his life now for complications. He was in Miragansett to settle his brother's affairs and that was all.

But for the first time ever, he wished he'd seen a certain woman before Jordan had.

Laura paced the gallery in anticipation. It was almost four o'clock. She kept an eye on the road from the big plate-glass window. The gallery was empty of customers at the moment. Heather was at the counter, tallying the day's receipts. For a Wednesday, they'd done well.

"You're going to wear a hole in the carpet," Heather murmured.

Laura glanced at her assistant. She had her head bent over the adding machine, but she peeped up at Laura and laughed. "You almost act as if you're going on a date."

"No. I just don't want him to have to hunt for parking. When I see him, I'll zip out and we'll be on our way." She took a deep breath. Jed was just a man on a mission. She was not going on a date. But the nerves that jangled could be confused for anticipation. She wasn't sure she should be doing this. But she was anxious to see him again. After the conversation last night she felt she knew him a little better.

"Right," Heather said.

"Really," Laura insisted, knowing she was keyed-up to see Jed again. Which was silly. He looked exactly like Jordan. She'd had enough of Jordan's antics. How could she look at Jed and not see his brother? It was confusing. Yet she knew there was a difference. She could feel it, despite the identical faces.

A nondescript white car slowed in front of the gallery. She spotted Jed driving.

"Lock up," she told Heather as she pulled open the door and hurried outside.

Jed saw her and stopped. Fortunately the traffic behind him didn't seem to mind. She quickly got into the car and he sped away.

"Parking is a bear on the island," he said. "I didn't realize since the hotel has plenty of spaces."

"It's usually easier to walk everywhere than find parking. Especially in the summer. Come November and you'll see a completely different side to things."

"Cold, I bet."

"We do get snow."

"Which way do we go?" he asked.

Laura gave directions as they drove, gradually relaxing as the scenery sped by. Jed didn't talk much and she kept quiet herself. It had been easier last evening to talk on the phone.

"Busy day?" he asked as they left the town limits and sped up along the highway. The tall stand of trees gave a rural feel to the road that connected two very busy towns.

"Yes, actually. Wednesdays are the days for special excursions for clubs and groups, and today turned out to be one for garden groups from all over the area. We had dozens of women in buying up all the floral paintings, and two even asked for future work from one of the artists."

"Do artists come to you, or do you go out searching for the next new talent?" he asked.

"Hugo built up a steady list of excellent artists. I try to keep them happy by selling their work. During the winter months, the gallery is closed several days during the week so I can make trips to nearby towns and cities to search for new artists. I have some regulars from as far away as Quebec and Virginia. Most are local to the areas of Massachusetts and Rhode Island or Connecticut."

"So you combine mini vacations with searching for new talent."

"Yes."

Laura had been burning with curiosity ever since Jed mentioned the women's clothing last night. What had he done with it? Did he suspect the truth when she'd blurted out they weren't hers?

Maybe the woman she'd discovered in bed with Jordan had not been a one-time deal like he'd said. Would it have mattered if he'd been seeing her longer? Jordan had not taken their breakup well. She'd not taken it so well herself. Was there something lacking in her that he'd turned to another woman? Had her decision been so hard to take that he'd been careless the next day? Drinking to excess and then speeding until he crashed?

She would not dwell on that. She'd done what she'd thought was right, what she had to do to keep her own self-respect. She was not responsible for Jordan's accident.

She kept telling herself that, though she didn't always believe it.

"Turn here and head for the center of town," she said some time later as they approached Provincetown.

The larger Cape Cod town looked similar to Miragansett. The New England saltbox houses were weathered from the centuries of use. The main street buzzed with activity, giving every evidence of the summer tourism boom. Prim brick shops with old-fashioned signs displayed from the facades blended with some newer buildings made of glass and concrete.

"Turn left here and go up three blocks, then we'll turn left again. Then right and then left. It's on a dead end street," she said, pointing to a street that climbed a slight hill.

Jed drove the short distance, turning into in the parking lot of the thrift shop a few moments later. Colorful flags fluttered over the entrance to the shop. The parking lot was half full. He parked and unloaded the several bags. Laura sat in the car, watching him as he gave away his brother's clothes. It had to be hard. She'd been fortunate in her life not to have to deal with death before this. Her grandparents, all four, were alive and well. Her parents were in great health. No friends had yet died.

Only an ex-fiancé. And only she knew about the ex part. It would help no one to tell of their breakup and she felt it would hurt Maria. So Laura kept the secret from all except her best friend.

"All set," Jed said, getting back into the rental car. "Too early for dinner, want to show me Provincetown? Or do you need to get back?"

"I have time. Provincetown is a lot like all the other Cape Cod towns, only bigger. I know a place where we can find shaded parking."

Soon they parked beneath a huge maple, on a residential street not far from the harbor.

Jed studied the houses as they headed for the center of town, commenting on the architecture and ornamentation. Some were bleak, weathered wood, no trim. Others had been painted, cared for and dressed up. Gardens abounded everywhere, hollyhocks and gladiolas bobbing in the wind, snapdragons and roses spilling color of every description.

When they reached the main street, Jed guided her around a group of teenagers too busy listening to music and laughing to keep the sidewalk clear.

"They could take that elsewhere," he said.

She nodded. "But they're just kids. If they can't be at the beach, there's not much more for them. I know what it's like. The town in Iowa I grew up in is small, not much to do for farmers' kids."

"Tell me about Iowa," he said as they strolled along.

"Not much to tell."

"I felt that way about bridge building, yet I talked your ear off last night."

"And I enjoyed every moment," she said, surprised to realize how fast the evening had gone. She had enjoyed it. She glanced at him, startled afresh at how much he looked like Jordan. If she didn't look at him, she could imagine he was someone totally different. But seeing his face, she was instantly reminded of Jordan. And the hurt he'd caused.

"So would I like hearing about you," he said. "We were almost related."

She glanced up, caught in the snare of his dark gaze. For a long moment Laura felt as if the world was fading. It was hard to breathe, to swallow. That constant flare of attraction startled her and for a shocked moment she wished things had been different—that she'd met Jed Brodie first and never known Jordan. What made her so sexually aware of this man? Was it his looks, so like Jordan's? Could she never escape the snare of falling for this face? Jed seemed so little like Jordan. Or was he? She hadn't really known Jordan after all those months, how could she know Jed after two days?

She was jostled by a passerby and quickly stepped aside. She refused to read anything into Jed's comment. Or the heated look in his eyes.

CHAPTER FOUR

LAURA tried to treat their outing like a native showing a visitor around, pointing out the different tourist spots of Provincetown. It worked better if she kept her distance and didn't keep trying to see Jordan in Jed. Her feelings were too confused to make sense. She was angry at Jordan, hurt—and attracted to his brother. She led the way purposefully, hoping to outwalk her thoughts.

They ended up at the water's edge. Late swimmers were still enjoying the water. Not dressed for the beach, Laura compromised by kicking off her shoes and walking barefoot on the sand. The breeze blowing from the water cooled. Before long the tumbled thoughts eased and she could look at things dispassionately. Jed was a visitor; he'd be leaving soon. She could do this.

Shortly after six, Jed suggested an early dinner. She offered the choice of a quiet restaurant known for its seafood on Main Street or one right on the water, similar to Sam's Shack in Miragansett.

Jed chose the waterside one. "I want to be near the sea as much as I can while I'm here," he explained.

Laura hadn't been out to dinner in months except with her friend Sally. No one wanted to invite a grieving fiancée. Another reason to tell the truth. But she didn't want to needlessly hurt the Brodies. It was too late to announce to the world their breakup. Sally knew, but no one else did. She and Laura had been close friends almost since the day Laura moved to Miragansett.

When their order had been taken, Jed settled back in his seat and looked at her. "What do you do when you are not working?" he asked. "Hobbies?"

She looked at him warily. "Why?"

He shook his head, his eyes lit in amusement again. "You're distrustful, now I wonder why? Can't I be simply curious?"

"A small business owner seems to be working all the time," she said with a rueful smile. "But when I do break away, I love to swim and sail. I'm part owner in a small sailboat. It's an extravagance, but one I splurge on. Iowa has no sea, obviously, and I love sailing. One of my friends, Sally Benson, got me interested several years ago. We took lessons together right after I moved here and then decided we wanted to keep sailing. So we first bought an old boat, had great fun in that, but moved up a couple of years ago to the one we have now."

"Adventuresome," he murmured. "Did you and Jordan sail together?"

"Of course. We talked about getting a boat of our own once we married. Do you sail?"

"Did a little in college. And when I was working on a project in Indonesia. Haven't been on a boat in ages, unless you count the barges we use to transport materials to the work site up the Amazon."

"That's an amazing river."

"Not fresh and clean like the sea, however. I can see the appeal of living in Miragansett to my parents."

"Yet they rarely go out on the sea. They're consumed with their art," Laura said. "Jordan hadn't understood that part. He loved the water, loved other activities."

Jed nodded. "We used to vacation on Nantucket Island when we lived in Boston. You couldn't get either of us out of the water unless it was for food." He fell silent as if remembering happier days when he and his brother had been close.

Laura wished she'd known both men as boys. Maybe it would have given her some insight into the relationship.

While they ate, talk turned to impersonal topics such as books read and movies seen. As far as recent films were concerned, Jed was behind the times because of his work out of the country. But he read a lot. Laura did, as well, during the winter months, and she was taken aback to discover they both enjoyed cozy mysteries. She would have thought his tastes would run to adventure novels.

"I'd think you'd want to blow off steam after a hard week at work and head for the nearest town to celebrate, not read," she said at one point.

"If you mean take a boat fifty miles down the river to a port town to find a bar for some liquid refreshments, and then try to get transportation back up river in time for work, that's not for me. Some men do it, but drinking in the tropics is hell. I'd rather save my time and money for when I can get to a large city, with time between jobs. I don't drink much. Can't have it on the work site. I guess a person gets out of the habit after a while."

Another difference between the brothers.

She had to stop comparing them. Jed was going to be around for a few days. They'd work together to wind up Jordan's estate and then never see each other again.

The next afternoon promptly at two, Laura turned into the driveway of Jordan's cottage. She'd done so many times before—the last time being the day she'd surprised him in bed with another woman. Cutting the engine, she sat without moving for a long moment. Memories assailed. How she'd been so crazy about Jordan's attention she'd rushed here from work many evenings, thrilled to see the man she loved.

At first he'd seemed to be everything she'd want in a

husband. But as the weeks slipped by, she realized his lifestyle and values were too different from hers to make a lifelong commitment. But she could still remember those heady first days of falling in love.

Sighing for what might have been, she got out of the car and walked to the front door. Knocking, she waited. Jordan had given her a key, but she didn't feel right using it today. In fact she planned to return the key and her engagement ring to Jed. Jordan had refused the ring that fateful afternoon. He'd begged her to keep it, hoping she'd change her mind. She knew she would not have.

She blinked back tears. The shock and devastation of that day swept through her again. She wasn't sure she wanted to go inside. It would be better to just get back into her car, drive away and come up with some excuse as to why she could not do this.

Jed opened the door. He wore worn khaki slacks and a dark blue T-shirt. A blast of cool air swept over her.

"Come in. It's too hot to stand outside," he said, stepping aside to open the door wider.

"It's cooler by the water," she said, stepping into the cottage. Odd—it looked the same. She had changed so much since that afternoon, she half expected the cottage to look different. For a moment she expected to hear Jordan greeting her.

Jed closed the door. "Can I get you an iced tea before we tackle the paintings?"

"Sounds good," she said.

Laura followed Jed into the kitchen. It was spotless. But empty, no longer Jordan's.

"You've been busy," she said as she waited for the beverage.

"Gives me something to do. I've cleared out most of his bedroom and bath. Mom said she'd rented this place furnished for him, so most of the furnishings aren't his. She's still paying rent, but once we're done, she can stop."

"It's hard being here today," Laura said as he handed her a frosty glass of iced tea, keeping one for himself.

"I read the police report. His alcohol level was sky-high. There were maybe a dozen bottles of booze here, most empty. He had a drinking problem, didn't he? More than just a party guy."

Laura hesitated, taking a sip of the cool drink, stalling. Finally she nodded. The truth couldn't hurt Jordan any longer. "I thought he had a problem anyway. We fought several times over it. He said it was just letting off steam. No harm. Ironic, it was what killed him."

Jed nodded as if in confirmation of something he suspected. "He drank in college, as well. I thought he'd cleaned up his act. Guess some things are hard to change. You know where the paintings are?"

"In his studio. I think that's the reason your mother rented this place for him. It has that large lovely room with the northern light and bank of windows."

They didn't have to pass the bedroom to reach the studio. Laura was glad. It felt strange to be walking around the house knowing Jordan was gone forever.

The studio looked as it had the last time she'd seen it. Jordan had been so proud of his body of work, as he called it. Pointing out aspects as if she couldn't see them for herself. Canvasses were stacked all around the room. Some on end, others lying flat. The room was cool and smelled of oil paints and thinner.

"So, do we inventory every one and then you take your time appraising, or work on one at a time?" Jed asked, surveying the chaotic room.

"It's not going to take that long to appraise them," she said. Taking a large tablet from her carryall, she put the bag on the floor and searched for a pen. She also withdrew a small marker pen.

"We'll number the upper left corner of the back of the canvas to keep them straight. We can't call all of them Seaview from Miragansett."

He looked at the top painting in each stack. They all appeared similar, and the description she made would fit each one.

Laura looked around and decided to start on the left side and work her way around the room. She doubted she could get half done today. But she'd get nothing finished just standing around.

She picked up the first one, marked it with a 1 on the back, and then studied it, turning it to the light.

"So how do you appraise it?" Jed asked, coming to stand beside her.

"For someone who has never sold anything, I would just give it what I think its fair market value is." She glanced up at him. "I could be wrong, you know. It could be once these hit the market, people will flock to buy them."

He studied the painting and slowly shook his head. "I don't think so. This one is not all that good. He didn't even cover the canvas here," Jed said, pointing to an area near the left side where the white canvas showed.

She felt awkward. She had to be totally honest, her own reputation as an art dealer rested on that one factor. But she hated letting Jordan's family down. Maria was going to be so unhappy.

She put the painting down and jotted a note on the pad. Maybe when she totaled it all, it wouldn't seem so bad.

"That's not efficient. It'll take twice as long that way. Let me do the writing, you examine the paintings and dictate what you want to say," Jed said, reaching for the notepad.

His hand almost closed over hers as he took the pad. She felt a flash of awareness at his touch. She almost jumped back.

He looked at the figure noted and then at the painting.

"My mother is going to be in for a major disappointment. You're right with what I've seen so far. The ones at your gallery are the best."

"I'm counting on what you said—that your mother is honest

about art and not seeing what's not there because Jordan did the paintings."

The cooperative effort worked well. Laura spent several minutes on each picture, trying to envision them in appropriate frames, meeting the needs of visitors to the Cape. Even allowing for top dollar, she was not appraising them high. And many of the paintings were incomplete—as if Jordan had reached a point where he got bored and moved on to something else. Those were virtually worthless.

Every time she gave an estimate, she glanced at Jed. He showed no expression, calmly writing down the number, a brief description she voiced and appraised value. Jordan would have grown bored and tried to talk her into something more fun. And she would have given in, she knew. He had that way about him.

Jed's stoic manner was starting to make her nervous. She looked at another painting. Not all were of seascapes. Jordan had done several classic still lifes and some portraits. When she came across the nude, she recognized the woman as the one she'd found with Jordan that afternoon.

She had forgotten this was here. She'd gone through all the pictures when Maria insisted on the retrospective. She'd taken the best of the lot. She'd wanted to burn this one, but, of course, had not. She couldn't bear to look at it.

Jed looked at that picture and then at Laura.

"It's not me," she said.

"I can see that. Some model?"

Laura shrugged, moving on to the next painting. The entire process was going quickly. She was speeding up trying to get through the afternoon. The longer she was around Jed, the more nervous she became.

The light was fading when Laura called a halt. They had done more than half.

"Are these all?" Jed asked.

"As far as I know," Laura said. She leaned the last picture

against the stack, and surveyed how many more remained. "I can finish tomorrow afternoon if you like." The sooner she finished the sooner she could escape Jed's presence.

"After he left college, Jordan declared he'd become a painter. I'd have expected more from almost twelve years of work. How long does it take to do one painting?"

"It doesn't matter now. He's gone."

Jed looked at her. "I'm sorry. This has to be hard for you."

She shook her head. She didn't want more sympathy. The time for sympathy was when she found out the man she thought she'd marry had cheated on her.

"I need to get going," she said, wanting to flee the memories being here brought.

"Have dinner with me. I'm on leave from work for the first time in five years. I've just lost my brother. My parents are grief-stricken and don't want my company. They say it's too hard looking at me and seeing Jordan. Do you feel that way?" In his world, no one knew his brother, so no one drew comparisons. But here, he was the outsider, he was the one who looked like the favorite son—but wasn't.

Still, being with Laura brought him closer to Jordan. He had not had a chance to say goodbye. Had his brother known the car was crashing? Had he tried to swerve and avoid the fatal tree? He couldn't believe he'd died three months ago and he'd only just learned about it. Shouldn't he have felt the world change when Jordan died?

"Okay. I need to change, though. These are old clothes for grubbing around in the studio."

"Shall I pick you up in say thirty minutes?" he asked. He'd ask at the hotel about a nice place. Make it a nicer dinner than last night.

"Make it an hour. I'll leave the tablet here. You remember the way to my place?"

He nodded. He'd dropped her off when they returned from

Provincetown. Miragansett wasn't a very large town, and the streets were neatly laid out in squares. "I'll find it again."

Once in her car, Laura let the doubts rise. This would be their second dinner together. She wasn't reading more into it than warranted, was she? He was lonely. She could tell him about his brother's last days. He had no idea how hard it was to keep talking about Jordan when she wanted to rail against him for ending things as he had. Still, Jed was family and she knew he needed some closure.

Not that it was her goal in life to comfort Jed Brodie. She could think of other things she'd rather do with the man.

Shocked at her wayward thoughts, she started her car and hurried home. She would be calm, friendly and make sure tonight was the last dinner she shared with him! He looked too much like Jordan for her. She was getting her emotions mixed up. Just because he looked like Jordan didn't mean he was like him—either in wanting a relationship with her, or in being untrustworthy.

Jed was surprised at his own reaction after the afternoon with Laura. He'd just lost his brother, but they had not been close. For the last decade he'd all but severed ties with his family. There was no changing that now, much as he wished he'd done things differently. Being with Laura was a link to Jordan.

She was more than just a link, however. She intrigued him despite that air of sadness surrounding her. He knew she was recovering from the loss of his brother. But it didn't stop him wanting to have her look at him. To see him as a separate man. He knew he looked like his brother. Would she forever see Jordan each time she looked at him?

Tonight he'd make her see that he was *not* Jordan. He was very different, in every way. He was still young and healthy. While he hoped to remain that way for a long time, there were no guarantees in life. Building large structures in foreign countries wasn't without risk. He wanted to date, maybe fall a little in love, do things totally different from what he had been doing. Jordan's death had been a wake-up call.

Ever since he'd had to deal with the mess Jordan caused in college, Jed had avoided his brother and his friends. Laura was different. He was tired of playing second fiddle to Jordan. She was someone he could become interested in. Maybe even see a future together. Could she ever feel that way about him?

The restaurant was elegant. The cloths covering the tables were pristine white and set with heavy silver and crystal goblets at each place. A small dance floor at the far end added an unexpected festive feel to the restaurant, without taking away from the ambiance of the rest of the establishment. Background music played softly until the orchestra came on at nine.

Laura again wore a summery dress. He liked the way she wore feminine clothes; that she didn't mind looking like a woman. He wasn't sure that was her persona for the gallery, but he liked it. There were four women on his crew in the Amazon, who wore the same kind of clothing the men wore.

Jed shook his head. He definitely needed a break if he was starting to notice women's clothing.

"Have you eaten here before?" he asked.

"Once or twice," Laura said, perusing the menu. "I'll have the sea bass."

"I'll have the lobster," Jed ordered a moment later when the waiter appeared to take their choices.

"Did Jordan bring you?" he asked.

"No. We never came here. This really isn't Jordan's kind of place. Wasn't, I mean."

"What was?"

"Barney's on Atlantic Avenue," she said, naming a nightclub that catered to the younger crowd. "He liked to dance and sing karaoke."

"Jordan sang?" Jed tried to picture that. He smiled in amusement. He remembered hearing his brother singing in the shower when they were teenagers. He had a terrible voice.

She smiled back. "You don't do that much. Smile. Jordan was always smiling and laughing."

"Just trying to picture my brother singing in public. Was he any good?"

"Not at all. But after a few beers, he thought he sounded like Mick Jagger," Laura said.

"Do you like Barney's?"

"Occasionally. Not as much as he did. I'm usually tired after working all day. I'm on my feet a lot with the job, both in the gallery and in the framing room, so my favorite spots are more quiet, soothing maybe. Great, that makes me sound like my grandmother."

"No, I know what you mean. Weekends are fun for going to nightclubs. During the week, a calmer place might be more suitable," Jed said.

She nodded. "Or staying in."

He glanced at the dance floor, wondering if he should ask her later. He looked at her trying to gauge her reaction to his choice of restaurant. Recommended by the clerk at the hotel, it seemed quite nice to Jed.

"Would you be up to dancing later?" he asked.

She shrugged. "Probably. I love dancing. I don't guess I'd ever be too tired for that." She smiled again, her gaze drifting around the room.

Jed wondered if he was imaging things, or had she rarely met his eyes since he picked her up?

"Tell me something," he said, waiting for her to look at him. She did. "What?"

He almost asked what she'd seen in Jordan. But he suddenly didn't want to introduce his brother into every conversation.

"How did an Iowa girl end up in college in Boston?"

"One thing most Iowa farm girls have in common is the desire to leave. Farming is great for my dad. And my mother loves putting up vegetables and fruits. She helps outside, as well. But that wasn't for me. I've always loved art. When one of my grandmothers took me to a gallery in St. Louis one time, I was captivated. So combining my desire to leave Iowa behind and study fine paintings and other works, I applied to a school in Boston and one in San Francisco. The one in Boston accepted me first."

"Otherwise you might be in California right now."

"That's right. Maybe. I love the history of this area. Ours in Iowa doesn't go back that far, you know."

"What was the first thing you remember doing when you arrived in Boston?" he asked.

Laura told him about her first year, how she'd played tourist every second she could. The talk veered back toward personal preferences and places they'd both seen. He took a lot of historic locations for granted, having been raised in the old city. She chided him for not appreciating everything more than he did.

Dinner was served and the conversation continued. By the time they'd each had a piece of cheesecake for dessert, Jed felt they'd made strides in forming a friendship of a sort.

It was enough for now.

A small orchestra began to assemble on the dais to the right of the dance floor. In only a few moments the slow rhythm of an old familiar song filled the restaurant.

"Care to dance?" he asked.

"Of course."

She went into his arms as if they'd danced a hundred times before. The floor was not crowded, though several other couples joined them. Jed drew her closer, relishing the feel of her soft curves against his body. She smelled of some light fragrance, like some elusive flower he couldn't quite name. Her hair was soft against his cheek.

"I love this song," she murmured, leaning back slightly to look up at him.

A spike of desire hit so hard it stunned him. He wanted this girl who had belonged to his brother. He wanted her more than any other woman he'd ever known.

Without thought, he leaned closer and kissed her. For a moment Laura didn't move, then she responded, moving her lips against his, opening to him. Her tongue danced with his as they circled the dance floor. If they'd been alone, he'd have deepened the kiss and caressed her in intimate places. But a modicum of rationality remained and he knew they were in a public place. One, moreover, where Laura was known. Reluctantly he pulled back.

She was breathing hard. So was he for that matter. He stared into her eyes, seeking for some sign she didn't regret the kiss.

She smiled tremulously and rested her forehead against his chin, still dancing.

He wouldn't say a word. What could he say? That he regretted kissing her? That would be a lie. That he wouldn't do it again? Another lie. If the opportunity arose, he wanted to give her more than a kiss on a dance floor. Much more.

CHAPTER FIVE

LAURA was sitting at her desk sipping a latte staring off into space the next morning when Heather came into the office. She closed the door and leaned against it dramatically.

"I just heard. What are you doing?" she asked incredulously.

Laura blinked and looked at her assistant. "Drinking coffee?" she offered.

"Last night, major clinch scene at the Pelican Restaurant. Half the town knows by now."

"It was just a kiss," Laura defended. Not true, of course. It could never have been classified as *just* anything. It had been amazing. Dreams could be built on such a kiss, if she weren't too levelheaded to know nothing could come of it.

"Did he remind you of Jordan?" Heather wanted to know.

"Not at all." What he reminded her of was the Jordan who might have been. Before her eyes were opened and she discovered him as he was. Laura didn't think she could explain that too well. In fact, she couldn't explain any of her feelings clearly. She wasn't sure she could clarify them to herself.

Guilt played a part. Should she be kissing anyone so soon after Jordan died? Even though she'd broken their engagement, she'd cared for him. She mourned the loss of the love she'd thought she'd have forever. Was she ready to move on to another? She was afraid to find out. What if the next man wasn't for her, either? Would that cause heartache to add to that she already had? A right-thinking person would take time to come to terms with what had happened.

Yet she felt an excitement around Jed she was not expecting. He made her feel thrillingly alive. Last night's kiss had startled her, caught her totally by surprise. And so had the rightness of it.

Or was she confusing him with Jordan?

She took another sip of coffee, wishing she was not having this conversation with Heather, it only brought up more questions than she had answers for.

"Are you going to see him again?" Heather asked.

Laura nodded. "To finish the inventory of Jordan's paintings. But that's all—I think."

"So no more dates."

"Last night wasn't really a date. We just went to dinner together," Laura explained.

"And danced and kissed enough that gossip is running rampant among the locals. I'm sure Maria and Jefferson will hear it before long."

"Oh, jeez," Laura moaned. There was always a downside to living in a small community, even one which swelled with tourists in the summer months. "It was just a kiss, dancing and all. I know it meant nothing to Jed Brodie. Let's forget about it, shall we?"

"If you can. Don't say I didn't warn you if we have a lot of curious browsers today, each wanting to talk to you to see if anything will slip. It would be so romantic. You lost Jordan, but found his twin. Are they indistinguishable?"

"Good heavens, no. As you've seen, he looks like his twin, but Jed is totally different from Jordan." Was she getting the two of them confused? Was she trying to find a connection to replace the one severed by Jordan's betrayal?

No. She knew the difference. The brothers were not interchangeable.

Jed was a hard worker, had already risen fairly high in the construction world to be in charge of such mammoth building sites like the one in the Amazon. His superiors depended upon him, as did all the men and women who worked for him. Was he the kind of person who would cheat on a new fiancée? She didn't know him that well, but something told her Jed Brodie would never do such a thing to someone he professed to care for.

"Well, it could be romantic."

"Heather, I have no interest in Jed Brodie beyond working with him to wind up Jordan's estate. If anyone really needs to see me, do come get me. But you handle any gawkers."

"Sure thing, boss." She laughed softly and slipped back into the gallery.

Laura shook her head. She so did not need further complications.

She finished the tax forms she was working on and cleared her desk so she could move to the framing room. She enjoyed the variety of tasks needed to run a successful gallery.

No sooner had she begun to frame a new acquisition than Heather popped her head in.

"Maria Brodie is on the phone for you," she said.

Laura sighed and put down the frame. "I'll take it here," she said, moving to the extension.

"Good morning, Maria, what can I do for you?" she said in her very best professional voice.

"I've heard a disturbing rumor and you can set the record straight," Maria said without preamble. "You and Jed dined out last night and were kissing and dancing for hours. I can't believe the rumors people spread. How preposterous."

"Which part?" Laura asked carefully. She did not need Maria's interference.

"That you'd be dating so soon after Jordan died for one thing. And to go out with Jed would be beyond anything. He's Jordan's brother. He should have more sense."

"We went out for dinner, Maria. He kindly offered to buy me a meal after we worked on appraising Jordan's paintings yesterday afternoon."

"At the Pelican?"

"Apparently the hotel recommended it."

"Dancing? Kissing?" Her voice sounded horrified.

"We danced a couple of times after our meal. Maybe there was a brushing of lips," Laura said, trying to minimize things. It wasn't as if she owed Maria any explanation. But she felt compelled to respond though she didn't need to justify herself to Jordan's mother.

"Laura, do you think that's wise? You had a terrible shock when Jordan died. I know Jed looks like him, but he's not Jordan. I know you loved my son. We all did. Don't confuse them."

Laura knew it was the grieving mother speaking, but she was suddenly defensive and annoyed that Maria thought she had the right to talk to her this way. She had tried to protect Jordan's memory by not mentioning that last afternoon to his parents. Maybe that had been a mistake.

"I am not confusing them. Jed likes to talk about Jordan. They were twins, close at one time, he says. Over the last few years other commitments kept them apart. I think he enjoys hearing what I can tell him about Jordan."

In fact, that could be the only reason he spent time with her. The thought made her vaguely depressed.

There was silence for a moment. Then Maria spoke in a strained voice. "It's just so soon after Jordan died. I'd think his memory deserved more respect."

"His memory deserves all the respect we can give it," Laura said gently. "Jed and I are not doing anything to disrespect that. Jed is your son, too. He grieves for Jordan's death."

"I miss him so much," Maria said before Laura could say any more. "He was the sweetest little boy. Always so affectionate. And talented. I can't bear to think of his being gone forever."

"Jed's being home must bring you some comfort," Laura said. She didn't understand the Brodies. If she'd had a family member die, she'd want the rest of the family close by to offer comfort, and to remember together.

"Jed never understood his brother."

Or maybe he understood him all too well, Laura thought with sudden insight.

"I should have known that you were not dating again. Now that you said it was a working dinner I understand better. But kissing Jed. My dear, I know he looks like Jordan, but I don't think that's wise."

"I didn't kiss him because he looks like Jordan." What a horrible thought. Surely Jed didn't believe that. "Put it down to the mood of the evening. Maria, we all miss Jordan."

"I know. And I for one shall miss him all my life. In time you need to move on. I know that, but not yet. It's too soon."

Laura made a noncommittal sound.

"How is the appraisal coming?" Maria asked in a bracing voice.

"I was able to complete about half yesterday afternoon," Laura said, glad for the change of topic.

"Half. Good heavens, are you spending enough time on each one? That seems quite fast to me."

"There aren't that many. I'd say we did about eighty yesterday. I'm more than half through."

"You must be mistaken. Jordan painted for years. Even given he was slow when starting there should be hundreds of paintings."

"There aren't at the cottage. Would he have some elsewhere?"

"I don't understand. There should be years worth of work." Maria repeated.

Laura had thought so herself before she suspected Jordan's method was to paint when there was nothing else to do.

"Maybe he was a perfectionist and destroyed work he didn't

consider good enough to keep," Laura suggested. She knew some painters did that.

"I'll have to talk with Jefferson. Jed is being quite unreasonable about following the terms of the will."

"His responsibility is to do so," Laura defended. Why wouldn't he? Sometimes she wondered about Maria's grasp of reality.

"We'll see how the showing goes," Maria said. "He's sure to see his brother in a different light after the opening."

Laura replaced the phone and wondered yet again if she should have told Maria and Jefferson everything about their relationship.

By late afternoon she had accomplished a great deal in framing the paintings she planned for Jordan's show. She was tired, but in a pleasant way. Heather had been spot-on with her predictions of more visitors to the gallery. She had fielded the curiosity. Sales had been up, and interest was growing about the retrospective of Jordan's work. Laura hoped pent-up demand would make it a stellar show for Maria's and Jefferson's sake.

She locked up at six and headed for home. Unless the weather was too awful, she normally walked the few blocks. Reaching her flat, she quickly changed and then went to the kitchen to see what she could throw together for dinner.

There was a knock at the door.

When she opened it, Jed stood there, dressed casually, large pizza box in hand.

"Dinner?"

She studied him for a long moment, wondering why he had showed up.

"Your timing is perfect. I was just gazing at all the things in the refrigerator wondering what would miraculously fix itself. I love pizza. But I'm a bit surprised to see you here."

"I called my folks, but Dad was in the studio and didn't plan to stop for something as mundane as dinner. Mom was lying down. She said she had a headache. I could tell by her voice she was feeling tired. So rather than eat alone in the hotel dining room, I took the chance you'd be free."

She stepped aside as he entered.

He glanced around her apartment and then looked at her, raising an eyebrow. "Where do we eat?"

"Since the balcony is too tiny to seat us both, it'll have to be the dining table. "I'll clear it off." It was cluttered with mail and magazines. She swept them into a pile and put it all on her coffee table. A quick scan of the room showed the rest was in passable condition for drop-in company. Had she known anyone was coming, she would have made sure the place was completely tidy.

"Have a seat and I'll get plates, napkins and something to drink. I have wine, beer or soft drinks."

"I'll have a cola if you have it," he said, putting the large box on the cleared spot of the table.

Laura got the items needed and returned in only moments. She wasn't sure how to take Jed's unexpected arrival. And she was disturbed by the burst of joy she experienced when she opened the door. She was trying to keep this relationship on an even, businesslike keel. She didn't have a single other business relation where the person showed up on her doorstep with pizza.

But his explanation sounded genuine. She couldn't imagine any ulterior motive.

When she returned, he was not at the table, but stood near the short hallway that led to her bedroom, studying one of the oil paintings on the wall.

"This isn't Jordan's," he commented.

The half falling-down, weathered wooden barn was on a lonely expanse of prairie. The painting captured the feeling of desolation and lost hopes.

"No." She pointed to a black-and-white pen drawing near the front door. "That one is, however. He gave me that on one of our first dates." The drawing was of an overturned rowboat, paddles nearby. Small, only about six inches square, it was a good pen-and-ink drawing.

"So who did the barn?" he asked, going back to that one.

"I did."

Jed looked surprised. "I didn't know you painted."

"I don't do much anymore. I'm not that good. I love being around excellent works of art, so running the gallery suits me better. So does the more regular income."

"You are good," Jed said. "Do you have others?"

"I only painted when I was younger. There are a couple in my bedroom. Mostly from Iowa, so they remind me of home."

"So what did you do all day?" she asked when they sat at the table. She was curious as to what he'd find to do in Miragansett. He must be so anxious to return to building that bridge.

They each served themselves. She poured two glasses full of cola and sat back to enjoy the pizza. The topping had everything but anchovies. The best kind, she thought taking the first bite.

"More of the same—packing up Jordan's things. I called a dealer to look at the few pieces of furniture that were his. They're not worth much. Nothing old enough to be an antique. Nothing new enough to command top dollar. Except for the paintings, I expect to have the place emptied of his things next week."

"And then you're leaving?" she asked.

"I'm not sure. A couple of days ago I'd have said yes. Now, I may want to stay around a little longer. If Mom can get by her seeing Jordan when she sees me, I'd like to spend a bit more time with my parents. It could be years before I can make it back."

"Stay for the show. I think your parents would be glad of your support for that."

"Dad came by the cottage to see me today." Jed took another slice of pizza and put it on his plate. He looked at Laura, his gaze catching hers. "He's in the midst of a new sculpture. His way of dealing with grief, lose himself in his work. We don't seem to have much to talk about."

"So why did he come?"

"Apparently he heard about our dinner last night."

Laura suspected where this was going. "And?"

"I know you're grieving for my brother. Was last night just about Jordan?"

"No." She couldn't say much more because she wasn't sure what last night had been about. She didn't want Jed to think he was a substitute for his brother—not with her or with his parents.

She looked at the pizza. "Was that the reason for pizza, so we wouldn't be seen in public while you asked me?"

Jed laughed aloud. "Nothing so ulterior. I like pizza and took a chance you would, as well."

"I should tell you it was a great day at the gallery because of everyone dropping by to glean what they could. Fortunately for me, Heather was there to field the inquiries."

"I've never lived in a small town before. Sounds like something I would not like," Jed said.

"It'll pass. Your being here is news. Your family is well-known and I think everyone is fascinated to see Jordan's image walking around."

"We looked alike. We were not alike," he repeated.

"I've figured that out myself," Laura said.

"I'm not out to antagonize my parents. They have enough to deal with. I wouldn't mind seeing your boat, however."

"That can be arranged. We could even take a quick sail today if you like. It'll be light for a couple of more hours," she said. Truth be told, she'd like to get out of the intimacy of dining together in her apartment. She found herself studying him as he ate, noting how his hair was cut, wondering if it felt as thick as his brother's. It was hard to look at him and not see Jordan, but gradually she was seeing Jed's personality stamped on his features. His own quiet ways, different from the flamboyance she'd dealt with before. She wasn't sure how she felt about it. It was so strange to see Jordan's features and hear different thoughts come from that mouth.

She gave Sally a call when they finished eating to make sure she didn't have plans for the boat.

"Not this week. Maybe I'll want to take it out next weekend. I was going to call you to see if you wanted to do an overnight up the coast."

"I'll see. I want to show it to a friend tonight."

"The same friend you were kissing last night at the Pelican?"

"Good grief, the rumor mill has been working if you heard it at work." Sally worked as a nurse at the local hospital.

"Which does not answer my question."

"Yes, I'm taking Jed Brodie to see the boat. Satisfied?"

"Might be. He anything like his brother?"

"No."

"Have fun."

Laura started to tell Sally it was only a kind gesture to a visitor, but conscious of Jed standing nearby, she refrained. "Thanks. Call me next week and we can discuss the trip."

She hung up and turned.

"We're all set. She doesn't have plans," she said, feeling a sudden awareness that had her heart pounding. Wiping her palms on her shorts, she stepped back. Was it her imagination or did Jed seem to take up more room in her apartment than other visitors?

The remaining pizza was wrapped and put in the refrigerator, the glasses in the sink, trash disposed of and they were off.

Walking down to the harbor, Laura was conscious of the curious glances they received. She wondered at the comments that would circulate tomorrow. The sooner they were on the boat, the better as far as she was concerned.

"This is it," she said with some pride when they reached the slip. It was a twenty-six-foot, single-masted boat, bobbing quietly in the slip.

The water was slightly choppy from the westerly wind. The sun was in the west, but would not set for another couple of hours.

"She's a beauty," Jed said.

"Sally and I think so. Come aboard." Laura stepped onboard and did a quick inspection, starting the blower to clear any gas fumes. When they were ready to leave, she looked at him.

"Can you swim? I have life jackets that I insist people wear if they can't swim."

"I can swim," Jed said.

"Okay, then. The jackets are in that compartment. I take a couple out to have on deck and readily available in case of an emergency. Not that we've had one yet. I want to be prepared."

She competently backed out of the slip using the single engine. Carefully keeping below the speed limit, she cleared the harbor.

"Good wind tonight," she said, cutting the engine and beginning to raise the sails.

"Can I help?" Jed asked.

"Sure, pull this line until the sail is fully extended." She handed him a jib line as she rapidly pulled on the mainsail. The boat quivered a moment as the sails flapped in the wind. Once the lines were secure, she spun around and set the tiller to take advantage of the wind. The boat seemed to leap forward skimming the water as if in a race.

Jed sat beside her on the narrow bench. Land fell behind them as they moved out into the bay.

"Isn't this great?" Laura asked. She raised her face to the sky, enjoying the freedom of the boat. Turning to Jed, she smiled broadly. "If I could, I'd sail every day. I'm so glad you brought dinner so I could thank you this way."

"Me, too." He leaned over to kiss her.

Laura didn't know what to do. Let go the tiller and throw her arms around Jed, or pull back and try to keep her distance. While she was deciding, Jed's kiss sparked an answering desire deep within. She turned slightly for a better connection. This was as close to heaven as she'd yet reached—sailing while kissing such an exciting man.

The boat waffled. She broke the kiss and trimmed the sail, turning into the wind again.

"I need to concentrate," she said, feeling flustered.

"Wouldn't want you to capsize us," Jed said.

"It's a reliable boat. We'll be fine. But I do need to pay attention."

Jed settled back to enjoy the ride.

Laura's blood was pounding. She'd thought the sail a better idea than staying in her apartment, now she wasn't so sure. They were of necessity sitting close due to the size of the boat. And if he kissed her again, she didn't think she'd put up much resistance.

Maybe this had been a bad idea.

But Jed made no move to kiss her again. She sailed outbound for about a half hour, then turned to head back. It would take longer to return tacking against the wind.

Once the tension eased from the kiss, she enjoyed the sail. It was just what she needed to keep things in perspective. Jed was leaving soon. There was nothing between them. Any feelings she thought she felt were probably because he looked so much like Jordan.

"Can you come tomorrow to finish the appraisals?" he asked at one point.

"Saturdays are our busiest day. We have all the weekenders in town, as well as the summer residents coming and going. And some locals actually shop at the gallery, as well. With the publicity I'm starting to generate for the retrospective, I'm hoping more locals will stop in."

"When then?"

"Sunday afternoon?"

"Around two again?"

"Yes." Laura thought about it. She could easily finish the appraisals on Sunday. Then she really had no further tie with Jed. Unless, maybe she could get him interested in the show and stay. He could help select frames.

She was really reaching now. She was the art expert, not Jed. Hadn't that already been a bone of contention between him and his parents?

Surprised she enjoyed her time spent with him, she hated to see it end.

When they reached the harbor, they dropped the sails, furled them, then headed in under power.

"Thank you, Laura," Jed said formally when they were tied up. "It's much more refreshing to sail the bay than up the Amazon." He offered his hand to help her to the dock. She took it, feeling the hard calluses from work. He was slow to release hers.

"Anytime," she said. Would they ever go out again? For a longer sail than just a quick run after dinner? She doubted it. Not unless she sailed to South America and up that river.

She nodded to a couple who moored their boat two slips down as they passed on the dock. She wondered if she'd hear about this tomorrow, as well. Didn't anyone have better things to do than speculate on her love life?

Hardly that. She wasn't in love with Jed. Not sure she was even in like. Though those kisses gave her some pause. She was lonely, hurt from Jordan's betrayal, and felt a renewed sense of her own femininity when a sexy man like Jed kissed her.

They walked back to her flat in the growing twilight. The summer evenings were warm enough to enjoy, cool enough to be pleasant without the heat of the day. Families were out on Harbor Street, enjoying the outdoor dining, or strolling alone with treats from the ice-cream parlor. Children ran and dodged in and out among the other pedestrians. Groups of teenagers hung out with music blaring.

"After work, we don't sit outside much because of the

insects," Jed said. "We have modified tents, with elevated wooden floors and canvas sides that can be rolled up for whatever breeze is passing through. Radio reception is rare."

"So mostly you read," she said, remembering what he said at dinner the other evening.

"That and woodworking. I make toys and furnishing for the children of my local workers. They don't have much as a rule and it keeps me busy."

She looked at him. "You are an artist. Do your parents know?"

"Woodworking as a hobby is not the same thing as being an artist," he repeated carefully.

"Counts in my book. What kind of toys?"

He described some of the pull toys for toddlers, the cradles and high chairs for both dolls and children.

"The best thing is the wood is so available. What we cut, we use," he finished.

"Do you have any pictures of your work?"

"No. It's not art, Laura, just toys for kids."

"I wasn't thinking of representing it, just curious."

When they reached her apartment building, she invited him in.

"Not tonight, but I'll walk up," Jed said.

When they reached her door, he leaned an arm against the jamb, looking at her.

"Thank you, Laura, for taking me out in your boat."

"I'm glad you came," she said, wondering if he'd kiss her once more.

He did—reaching out for her and pulling her closer. His kisses were special, no denying that.

She looped her arms around his neck and gave herself up to the pure enjoyment. It had been far too long since she'd been kissed like this. Like she was the most important thing in the world. She felt young, alive and sexy with feminine response to his masculine touch. She wanted more than kisses. She wanted the promise of love that had been hers for such a short time. The expectation of a coupling that would surpass her dreams.

As Jed's mouth left hers to trail kisses against her cheek, along her jaw, at that pulse point in her throat, she felt as if she were floating. It had been too long.

"Jordan," she murmured.

CHAPTER SIX

JED reared back as if slapped. For a moment he couldn't believe what he heard. *She thought he was Jordan.* Or was using him as some kind of substitute for his dead brother.

Laura opened her eyes, gazing up at him in horror. *"Jed."*

He pulled her arms down and stepped back.

"I'm sorry," she said.

"Yeah, well, I should have expected it, shouldn't I? It's too soon since his death for you to move on. I'm not a substitute, though, Laura."

He turned and walked away.

"Wait, please," she called after him.

He kept walking.

It wasn't the first time he'd been mistaken for Jordan. When they'd been kids, Jordan had often told people he was Jed to create mischief.

Jed hadn't liked it then, he didn't like it now. He was fooling himself that anything could develop between him and Laura. She'd forever see Jordan. It was good he found out. Saved wear and tear on the heart later.

He got into the rental car and returned to the hotel. He'd asked earlier to have his room changed if a seaview one became available. He no longer planned to stay that long. Tomorrow he'd see what steps he could take to wind up the estate with or without his being present.

With the rest of his leave, he'd visit some friends or find a cool mountain to visit for a complete change from the Amazonian jungle.

The message light was flashing on his phone when he entered his hotel room. Suspecting it was Laura with some apology, he ignored it. He poured himself a drink from the in-room bar and sat in the sole chair, gazing out the darkened window at the few lights he could see. Keeping his thoughts at bay, he ignored the anger that hovered at the thought of Laura's confusing the two of them. He'd known her less than a week. There was no deep emotional attachment.

He was confusing her kindness to Jordan's brother with a genuine interest in himself. She had not led him on. If anything, she was shy and hesitant. He was pushing. And he wasn't sure why. Was it merely a flare of attraction stronger than anything he'd felt before? There was no future for them even if she saw him apart from Jordan. He was committed to finishing that bridge and when it was complete, there were others to be built. She lived in this vacation resort town, had build her business here and it wasn't portable enough to take anywhere.

He frowned. Why was he thinking of a future, anticipating roadblocks where none would be needed. He was not falling for the woman who loved his brother.

He took another sip of his drink then decided to call it a night. The phone rang again. Jed glanced over his shoulder, but made no move to answer it. There was nothing to say.

Laura let the phone ring until it switched to the automatic message recording. She hung up. She'd already left a message. Leaving dozens wouldn't help if Jed refused to answer the phone or return her call.

She leaned her head back against the chair, anger at her stupidity flooding. How could she have said such a thing? She had not been thinking of Jordan, except to mourn the loss of the love she thought would be with her forever. She'd been kissing *Jed*. She knew that. Why had Jordan's name slipped out?

Maybe because Jed's kisses were much more affecting than Jordan's had been. She'd been questioning the difference. That excuse sounded dumb to her own ears.

Picking up the phone she dialed her friend's number.

Sally answered after three rings.

"Were you asleep?" Laura asked.

"Of course, it's almost midnight and I have to get to work tomorrow. What's up?"

"I made a colossal mistake tonight."

"Doing?"

Laura hesitated. She wanted her friend's advice. But she felt like an idiot admitting to what she'd done.

"When Jed kissed me I said Jordan's name."

There was silence on the line for a moment. Then, "Let me get this straight, you're lip-locked with the brother of your dead fiancé and when you come up for air you call Jordan."

"Not really. I mean, yes, that's what it looks like, but I wasn't really calling Jordan."

"The kiss reminded you of Jordan?"

"Not at all."

"Better or worse?" Sally asked.

"Much better."

"So maybe you had better stick to some pet name and leave first names behind. What were you thinking?"

"I wasn't. I don't know why I said Jordan's name. But Jed thinks I was using him as a substitute for his brother. He left angry. I don't blame him. I tried calling, but he's not answering. I left a message, but he hasn't called back."

"Think on it, Laura. What if he'd been kissing you like

there's no tomorrow and then murmurs another woman's name in your ear?"

"I would hate it," she said, depressed.

"Probably made worse because of the twin thing," Sally added. "No one knows Jed around here. Everyone knew Jordan. He's probably had to fend off comments his entire stay. Girlfriend, you need to do some major apologizing."

"I tried. He wouldn't listen before he left. Now he won't call me back. Don't just tell me what I should do, give me some hints on how to do it."

Sally gave the matter some thought.

"If it were me, I'd get up early, get some luscious breakfast from Callie's Café and surprise him in the morning."

"And if he won't open the door?"

"At least you'd have a great breakfast."

"I don't know."

"Hey, nothing ventured, nothing gained. Besides, you'll catch him off guard with early breakfast and get to see what he looks like first thing in the morning. Not all bad."

Laura laughed. "I'm sure he'll care less about making a good impression. He probably hates me."

"More likely he's hurt you'd confuse them," Sally said seriously.

"I didn't confuse them. Not really." Laura thought about it for a minute. "Maybe I should tell him the truth about Jordan."

"My guess is it wouldn't come as a huge surprise to Jed," Sally said drily.

"Um, maybe. It would to his mother, I think. That's why I didn't say anything. I didn't want to tarnish her memories of her son."

"You can't keep protecting Maria Brodie. She's a grown-up. It's her son. Let her deal with things the way they are, not the way she wants them to be."

"Oh, Sally, she lost him. She doted on him and he died. She'll never get over it. The least I can do is help ease the transition time."

"You're too nice, Laura. You don't really think this showing of Jordan's paintings is going to do any good, do you?"

"Sometimes I feel I let him down. In retrospect, I should have given him a show."

"At the time you had to think of the gallery's reputation. This retrospective will be a nice tribute, everyone will feel good, but no one's going to buy those paintings."

"Maybe not. But just putting on the show will help Maria and Jefferson, I know it. I can't imagine the pain of losing a child. I'm still grieving and I was so angry at him that last day I can't stand it. How much worse for a mother?"

"That's a reason I can understand. Go to bed. Get up early and woo the brother."

Laura laughed and bid her friend good-night. She didn't want to woo Jed. Or did she?

Laura hadn't needed Sally's example to make her feel bad. She knew Jed thought she was dreaming of Jordan. If he only knew the truth would it change things? Probably not. She was too wary of getting involved again with another man—especially one who looked exactly like Jordan. She'd lived with the cover-up for all these months, she wouldn't tell him now. It didn't matter. And her reasons stood, she didn't want to cause Maria any more grief.

She set her alarm early, wondering if she could go through with Sally's idea.

It was not yet seven when Laura knocked on the door to Jed's hotel room. Fortunately she knew the desk clerk and had told her that she was delivering something for Jordan's brother. The magic words. Laura still felt guilty when people were so solicitous about her loss. If they only knew.

The large basket Callie had provided was heavy. Laura hoped she didn't have to turn and leave without Jed even being tempted.

The door swung opened abruptly. "That didn't take long,"

Jed said. He was wearing a towel wrapped around his waist and drying his hair with another. He stopped abruptly when he saw Laura.

"I thought you were room service," he said.

"Sort of." She held up the basket. "Breakfast is served." She held her breath, hoping he wouldn't slam the door in her face.

"This is what the hotel serves up now?"

"No, this is what I serve. May I?" She could hardly keep her gaze from his broad chest. The skin was bronze and taut over his muscular chest. There were more differences between him and Jordan than he knew. She swallowed hard. So much tantalizing skin so early in the morning wasn't good for her equilibrium.

He stepped to one side and opened the door wide.

She walked in and over to the small table beneath the window. There was only one chair. One of them would have to sit on the rumpled bed. She looked away. That would not be her! On the other hand, if she sat in the chair, she'd have to face the rumpled bed, where she was sure to visualize Jed sprawled across it asleep. Did he wear pajamas to bed? Somehow she doubted it.

Try to focus, she admonished herself as she placed the basket in the center and began to withdraw the china and silverware Callie had insisted upon. She had been delighted with the early morning breakfast surprise and surpassed herself.

"I have eggs Benedict, hot coffee, some homemade cinnamon rolls and a fruit compote," she said as she withdrew the warming trays from the wicker.

Jed had not yet said a word. Glancing over her shoulder, she met his eyes.

"What's this for?" he asked.

"To make amends. I need to go on record I was not thinking of Jordan when his name slipped out. I was fully involved in the kiss you and I were sharing." It sounded lame when she said it aloud. She had rehearsed it all the way over. Darn it, would he believe her?

"No amends needed. It was not a big deal." He shrugged and headed for the bathroom. "I'll get dressed and join you."

That would give her a few moments to get some control of the situation, Laura hoped. His comment hadn't been very encouraging. And she suspected it had been a bigger deal to Jed than he was willing to admit.

She had everything set when he came back into the bedroom. She had opened the window to let some of the fresh air blow in before the heat of the day made it uncomfortable. She'd also debated making the bed, but that might have been a bit too personal.

Jed sat on the edge of the bed and called to cancel the breakfast he'd ordered. Then he drew the table closer, looking at the elaborate feast. "This is nicer than anything I've had in a long time," he said sincerely. He met her glance and inclined his head slightly. "Thanks."

"My pleasure." She waited for him to begin to eat before starting herself. The hot food had retained the heat in the warming tray. The fruit was icy cold. She was pleased with the way things had turned out. Now if this only mended fences.

Laura hoped Jed would initiate a conversation. She was afraid to say anything less the tenuous truce be broken. She did not want to talk about Jordan or his paintings or their parents. It left little to talk about, she realized with depressing recognition. Anything personal would be viewed as suspect. They'd discussed other topics at their other meals, why couldn't she think up something now?

The phone rang. Laura gave a brief sigh of thanks. At least the growing awkwardness could dissipate while he spoke on the phone.

It was his mother. She obviously asked what he was doing because he said calmly eating breakfast with Laura. Without any more explanation, did Maria think she'd stayed the night and now they were sharing breakfast? Laura was horrified. She shook her head at Jed.

"What?" he asked, covering the mouthpiece.

"Make sure your mother knows I just brought it by," she hissed.

Amusement danced in his eyes as he realized why she was telling him that. Without agreeing, he removed his hand.

"Mother, Laura and I are adults. I'm sure what we do in our free time is our own concern."

Laura gave a small groan. She could imagine what Maria was thinking!

"Now why would I want to do that?" he asked. He listened another moment then spoke again, "I'm not sure I'm staying for long."

Obviously Maria had a lot to say. Jed was silent for several moments, his eyes steady on Laura. She began to fidget. Eating was impossible.

"I'll come by this afternoon, then," he said.

When he replaced the phone, he returned to the table.

"So what did your mother say?" she asked.

"She seemed startled to learn you were here."

"Sure, the way you made it sound, I'm not surprised. You should have told her I brought breakfast early."

"Then she'd want to know why."

"Oh, like thinking I stayed the night is preferable to that?"

"We're both adults," he began.

"Maybe, but I'm not having my reputation dragged through the gossip mill to give you some kind of amusing way to string your mother along. She must be horrified."

"Are you supposed to forego dating because Jordan died?" he asked. "It's been several months."

"We're not dating. Much less anything more. But I bet your mother thinks so, doesn't she? You should have told her the truth."

"She didn't call about that. She offered me the cottage while I'm here," he said.

Laura put down her fork. "You've been here several days. Why now?"

"Apparently she's worried someone will break in to steal the paintings. I'm to be the guard."

Laura looked at him. She could tell he was amused. "Are you serious?"

"Don't you think it ironic? Mom couldn't wait for me to be gone since I'm not fawning over the paintings like she is, yet someone must have suggested the possibility of some summer visitors helping themselves to the inventory. She thinks they'd make a killing. We need to complete the appraisals and get a monetary amount set for probate," he said.

Back to business. At least he was talking again.

"So are you moving into the cottage to guard the paintings?" she asked.

"I haven't decided. I thought to head out pretty soon."

Probably because there was nothing around town for him to stay for. "I'd love you to stay for the exhibit," she said.

"Why?"

"To see it, of course. It will be the only showing of your brother's work."

He rubbed his cheek and chin. He had not had time to shave and the rasping noise could clearly be heard. Laura watched him warily.

"We'll see," he said at last.

It wasn't until they were sipping the last of the fragrant coffee that Laura began to relax and believe maybe Jed had accepted her apology. Not that he'd said anything. If anything he'd remained a bit distant. But she deserved that for her faux pas. She hoped they could recapture the camaraderie she thought was developing.

"I can come by today and finish the appraisals," she offered. She didn't want to wait until Sunday now.

"If I shift my stuff out there, I'll let you know. At least the cottage has a view of the sea. What's the point of staying on Cape Cod if all I'm looking at is trees?"

She didn't want him staying at the cottage. Visiting there would forever remind her of the day she found her fiancé in bed with another woman. But she dare not tell Jed. Not and keep Jordan's memory intact for his family.

When he put his cup down, she began to gather all the used dishes and utensils to return to Callie. The basket was soon packed and she had no reason to linger.

"I'll come by around two," she said, carrying the now lighter basket to the door.

"I'll let you know if that won't work," he said, walking to the door with her.

"See you then," she said brightly.

He studied her for a moment then nodded. "Thank you for breakfast. But last night was an epiphany. You are not over Jordan and I'm not ready for any kind of relationship. I have my work waiting and a long-distance affair can't last. Things happen for a reason, and I think last night was a clear warning. Let's keep our interaction on a business basis, shall we?"

"Of course. See you at two." Laura kept the stupid smile plastered on her face until the door closed behind her. Then let it slip. Maybe breakfast had mended fences, but not the way she wanted.

By two, Laura had decided to adhere to Jed's request to keep things purely business. She wasn't certain in her own mind if she was attracted to Jed or to the illusion that Jordan once offered. Was she looking for some kind of relationship that would give her everything she expected and not be one full of pitfalls and reality? Was she ready to trust another man with her heart? She didn't think so. Sally was the one always surging ahead, certain the current man she was dating was Mr. Right.

Laura was more conservative. And after Jordan's actions, doubly wary of trusting.

She arrived at the cottage with a determination to finish the work this afternoon and be out of Jed's way.

Jed met her at the door. He was dressed in the same khakis and polo shirt he'd donned that morning. He had shaved in the interim, she noted.

Laura greeted him calmly, belying the rapid increase in her heart rate. Without looking directly at him, she went right to the studio. It was as they had left it a few days ago.

"Same as before?" he asked, picking up the clipboard.

"Sure." She picked up the first picture, wishing she could rush through the job and get out. But she owed it to Jordan and her own sense of artistic integrity to do the best job she could.

Noting a number on the back, she studied the scene for a moment then began her assessment. It grew easier as they progressed. There was not a lot of difference in either the style, execution or composition of the paintings. It was as if Jordan found one scene he liked and replicated it whenever he felt like painting. She couldn't even tell how recently he painted the scenes.

It was growing late by the time the last canvas was valued. Laura set it back against the stack she'd been working on and looked at Jed.

"It'll take me a few days to get everything put into a format you can use for tax purposes. This is my professional opinion of the paintings' worth. You may receive more or less upon sale."

"Understood," Jed said.

"You may wish to ask another appraiser for his or her valuation."

"I trust you."

In this, at any rate. "Well, good. But another opinion might be needed for tax purposes since there is no track record from sales. If you have two or three independent appraisers giving you the same valuation, it will carry more weight with the

IRS." She held out her hand for the stack of notes. "I can recommend some local people if you like."

Jed handed her the tablet and moved to stand near the window, gazing out to the sea. "This is the view he painted over and over, isn't it?"

"Seems to be," she said, stepping closer. "If you have any pull with your mother, I suggest you get her to view the paintings before the exhibit. I think she's going to be disappointed in what she sees and I hate for that to be in a public venue."

"I have very little influence with my parents. But I will tell her."

"Fine, then, I'm off."

He turned and looked at her. For a second Laura thought he was going to say something. Ask her to stay maybe?

"Thank you for all the speedy work. Please bill the estate."

She inclined her head. She looked around. It was unlikely she'd return to the cottage.

She reached into her pocket. "I have this for you." She held out the key to the cottage and the sparkling diamond ring Jordan had given her and refused to take back.

Laura looked at the ring, feeling the weight of disappointment and betrayal. When he'd first given her this ring she'd been so in love, so full of hope. She'd never expected to have it all tarnished and ruined within weeks. She'd taken it off and held it out to Jordan that horrible afternoon. But he'd refused to take it. He'd wanted to talk to her, but not with that woman around.

Only, he'd died before they ever talked. Not that mere talking would have changed anything. She knew that.

Jed looked at her. "Jordan would want you to keep the ring," he said.

Laura knew Jed believed everything had been perfect with their relationship. Would he be shocked to learn she had tried to return it to Jordan that afternoon, hurt and angry? The blonde standing in the bedroom doorway with the sheet wrapped partway around her had watched. What had she felt like when

Jordan closed Laura's fingers around it and told her to keep it until she calmed down and they could talk? Laura shivered, almost feeling the others in the room. She didn't care what that other woman had thought. She only cared that her heart had been broken that day.

She shook her head. "No."

"Why not?" Jed asked, his instincts obviously on alert.

"We aren't getting married. Let his estate have it. I have to go." She put the two items in his outstretched hand and turned to quickly walk to her car. It would be a long time before she'd trust another man again after the way her supposedly devoted fiancé had cheated on her.

Grateful for the work ahead, Laura returned to the gallery. It would take several days to type up all her notes and finalize the appraisal. The sooner started, the sooner finished. And working would keep her thoughts away from Jordan. And his more disturbing brother, Jed.

Jed held the ring in his hand, gazing at the sparkling diamond. The ring suited Laura, a simple solitaire. Why was she giving it back? He would have thought a woman would keep the ring as a sentimental keepsake. He closed his fist around the small ring. He'd never found a woman to love. When he thought about it, one day he wanted a family. The kind where everyone loved each other and there were no favorites played. With the right woman, anything would be possible. It was finding her that might prove impossible.

CHAPTER SEVEN

MONDAY was the day the gallery was closed. Many other businesses in town were closed, as well. The weekenders had left, and the locals knew better than to plan on shopping. Laura liked working at the gallery those days because it was quiet. It gave her a chance to catch up on paperwork or give every painting and art piece a good dusting.

This Monday she had partitioned off the alcove with screens and was trying to decide how best to display Jordan's work. Laura tried one display and then another. She had to decide on the layout of the paintings, then get the lighting in place for best viewing advantage.

She had one wall done to her satisfaction when there was a knock on the front door. Couldn't the person see the Closed sign? Laura peeked around the screen shocked when she saw the woman standing on the sidewalk, knocking again. She had wavy blond hair, makeup that looked overdone in the casual setting of Miragansett. She wore very abbreviated shorts even for summer and a loose-fitting top, sliding off one shoulder. The last time Laura had seen her, she'd been wearing Jordan's sheet.

The woman cupped her hands against the glass and peered in. She saw Laura and motioned to the door.

Laura couldn't believe she was there, much less demanding

to come in. Whatever in the world was the woman doing trying to enter the shop?

"I'm closed," she mouthed, pointing to the sigh.

The woman rattled against the door, knocking again.

Sighing, Laura went to open. She did not need this, but better to talk to her in private than have her shout something from the sidewalk. Just because shops were closed today, didn't mean people weren't out.

She unlocked the door. Standing so it couldn't be opened very wide, she said, "I'm closed today. Can you come another day?"

"I don't want to buy anything, I want to talk to you. And I'm only here today. Tomorrow I'm back at work." She pushed against the door and Laura stepped to one side to allow her entry.

"Come with me," Laura said after she relocked the door. She led the way to her office, crossed to her desk and sat down. What in the world was this woman doing here?

"I'm Tiffany Barrows," the woman said, looking around and sitting on one of the guest chairs. "You didn't know my name, I think. But you knew Jordan and I had something going on. I heard there's going to be a showing of Jordan's paintings." She looked at Laura.

"That's right. Next week. It'll open a week from Friday and run for five days."

"They worth a lot of money?" Tiffany was tall and slender. Her long legs were tanned and shown to advantage in the shorts. Her hair was long, wavy and swirling artfully around her face. She would definitely appeal to men. Laura was curious why she'd shown up at the gallery. To find out about the paintings? The advance publicity had listed times and dates in the newspaper.

"Art is valued on what people will pay. Nothing of Jordan's has ever sold, so I can only give an estimated value. My professional opinion has been given to the executor of his estate." It really wasn't any of Tiffany's business. Laura wouldn't divulge confidential information to a stranger.

"I don't care about appraisals, what will they sell for?" the woman asked.

"The paintings aren't for sale," Laura said. Why was the woman approaching her? Laura was surprised to discover she felt very little either way about this person. She would have thought she'd be furious to meet her. But it was Jordan who earned her anger.

"If someone offers enough, everything is for sale," Tiffany said, jumping up to pace the small space. "I need to know if they will bring in some money. I went to Maria Brodie, but she wouldn't give me the time of day. You're my next hope."

"What does it matter to you how much they are worth?"

"Don't you recognize me?"

"You were with Jordan the day before he died." Laura was proud of how calm her voice sounded. She could still see Tiffany standing in the doorway wrapped in the sheet. After she'd discovered them beneath those sheets together. Jordan had been contrite, apologetic. But no explanation he could have given would have changed the facts.

"No wonder he wanted me, you sound so cold and unconcerned. I miss him!"

"You of all people know our relationship changed dramatically that afternoon." Laura felt inadequate. Tiffany had tons more sex appeal going for her. The contrast was dramatic. No wonder Jordan wanted her on the side. Would he have ever been satisfied in their marriage?

Now, for some reason Jordan's lover had sought her out. Curiosity demanded to know why. "So again, I ask, why is any of this important?"

"I'm pregnant with his kid. And I want my share of his estate for the baby. I don't make enough to support a child. The Brodies are loaded. My baby deserves some of that money."

Laura stared at her. Tiffany was carrying Jordan's baby? Good heavens. She was stunned with the news.

"Does Maria know?" she asked.

"She thinks I'm trying some scam. I went there first. Sheesh, she's gonna be the baby's grandma. You'd have thought she'd be thrilled. Instead she accused me of lying. Get real, with the ease of DNA testing these days, who would ever try to scam anyone? I hear Jordan's brother is in town. Twins have identical DNA so matching would be a snap. Maybe you should talk to her. She almost went bonkers when I did," Tiffany said.

"She must have been surprised to learn what you had to say," Laura said. She couldn't imagine Maria's reaction. The woman had no idea Jordan had been seeing Tiffany. So much for keeping the secret so Maria wouldn't be hurt.

"Obviously. I'm just asking for what's due Jordan's baby. How much is his stuff worth? His estate can give some to his child," Tiffany said, glowering at Laura.

"Then you need to talk with Jed Brodie. He's the executor of the estate." Laura wondered if he had any inkling what was about to hit. "He's staying at Jordan's cottage."

Tiffany paced the small office. "Are you going to challenge it?"

"I have nothing to do with Jordan's estate, you should know that. You were there when I ended the engagement," Laura said calmly. For the first time she began to see things in a different light. Thankfully she'd found out when she did. What if she'd married him and Tiffany showed up with a baby? She shivered at the thought.

"Yeah, well, don't think he was heartbroken. He was going to end it, once you gave him a show. He would have moved onto the big time and taken me with him," Tiffany said with bravado.

"As I said, Jed is staying at the cottage. You want to call him there?" Laura said. She would not get into an argument with Tiffany. For all she knew, the woman was right.

Tiffany stopped pacing and considered it. "Not if he's going to give me the runaround like his mother did. You come with me."

"What? I'm not going with you."

"I need you as a witness. You can tell him Jordan and I were an item. At least he'll have to pay attention. If he wants tests, I don't mind. But they have to pay for them. I'm not flush with money like the Brodies are. I just want what's right for my baby."

Laura shook her head.

"I'll call Jed for you. Tell him you're coming," she offered. It was more than she needed to do for Tiffany. She couldn't believe the nerve of the woman, showing up here. Yet, if she had been pregnant, wouldn't she have done everything she could for her baby?

"I'm not going there alone. Who knows what a strange man would do?"

"For heaven's sake, it's Jordan's brother. He isn't going to do anything but listen to you. Whether he does anything beyond that is up to him."

"Maybe the entire town needs to know that Jordan was cheating on you. How would you like that?" Tiffany asked, glaring at Laura.

"I would not. But it would hurt his family more. The family also related to your baby," she said. Had she kept quiet these weeks because of a desire to shield Maria and Jefferson, or to keep from becoming gossip herself? For the first time, Laura wasn't sure some of her keeping quiet didn't stem from wanting to protect herself.

For a moment Laura almost called her bluff. But then, she had no idea what Tiffany would do next. And the best way to avoid rampant rumors all over town, was to get her taken care of. Laura didn't want the gossip, and she was sure Maria and Jefferson would not, either.

"I said I could call."

"I want you there," Tiffany said stubbornly. "I know you hate me, but if you ever cared for Jordan, you would not want to hate his child."

"Not a very good argument. What if I were also pregnant?"

"Are you?" Tiffany looked startled.

Laura shook her head. "Very well, I'll go to the cottage and talk to Jed. Do you have a car?" Laura asked, rising. Best to get it over with.

"Sure. I'll drive."

"I was thinking you could follow me over. That way you wouldn't have to bring me back here when we're finished."

"I guess that would be all right," Tiffany said.

In less than ten minutes Laura pulled into the driveway of the cottage. Only a couple of days ago she'd mentally said goodbye to all memories, good and bad. Never expecting to return, she certainly hadn't thought she'd be coming back with Jordan's pregnant lover.

"When's the baby due?" Laura asked after knocking on the door.

"Five months."

"So Jordan never knew," she said.

"Naw. And let me tell you it was a shock to me. At least it'll arrive in the winter months. Tips aren't so great then. Can you imagine me big as a house and trying to hustle tips?"

"Are you a waitress?"

"Cocktail waitress at the Blue Diamond Resort," she said, naming one of the larger ones in Provincetown.

Jed opened the door. For a moment he looked at Laura, then at Tiffany.

"Something tells me I'm going to regret this, but won't you ladies come in?" he invited.

Laura walked past him, wishing she could say something to make it easier.

Tiffany looked at Jed with speculation, the smile wide on her face.

"Well, don't you look just like Jordan. I mean, I heard you were twins, but seeing you in the flesh is quite the thing. It's like Jordan's still here." She brushed against him as she entered, tilting her head almost flirtatiously. "I'm Tiffany."

"A friend of Jordan's undoubtedly," Jed said, closing the door and regarding Tiffany.

"A very close friend," she said.

He looked at Laura. "How do you know Tiffany?"

"We never actually met formally before today. She came to the gallery to see me. I think you should listen to what she has to say."

"I'm pregnant with Jordan's baby," Tiffany said bluntly.

Jed raised an eyebrow and studied her for another moment. "I probably should be shocked, but I'm only mildly surprised." He looked at Laura again. "Did you know?"

She shook her head. "Tiffany came to me because your mother didn't exactly embrace her with welcoming arms when she told her the news."

"Knowing my mother, she undoubtedly called you a liar and told you never to try to besmirch the good name of her son," Jed said to Tiffany.

"How did you know?" Tiffany asked.

"It's happened before."

"It has?" Laura was startled.

"Old history. So what is it you want?" Jed asked.

"Some money to help raise this baby."

"As far as I know, Jordan didn't have any money," Jed said.

Tiffany waved her hand around in an arc. "He had this place, that fancy car. He was an artist. His paintings must be worth something. He always said they were."

"This place is leased by my mother. The car was totaled, and my father held the insurance on it. So far the total appraisal of the paintings comes to very little. Of course, I would see that Jordan's child got a portion of the estate. But if you're looking for lots of cash, there isn't any."

"He threw money around like it was water," Tiffany protested. "What am I going to do if I can't get help? I don't make enough to raise a baby."

"He was a lavish spender," Laura added quietly.

"Then I don't know where he got it. I've reviewed his tax records for the last few years, he didn't make enough to spend lavishly. Unless he was subsidized."

"What does that mean?" Tiffany asked. Her flirtatious attitude had faded. Now she became concerned, worried.

Laura almost felt sorry for her. Obviously she'd thought Jordan rich as could be and wanted a portion of the wealth for her baby.

"My mother probably gave him money to spend. Maybe she'll do the same for your baby."

"Not likely." Tiffany looked at Jed and then at Laura. "She's already told me she thinks I'm a liar. If I have to, I'll get a lawyer and have him get me a share."

"I'd be happy to give you the name of Jordan's attorney. Yours could call him and they could hash it out," Jed said.

"You bet they can. A baby should get some of his father's estate."

Jed crossed to the dining room and grabbed a pad off the table. Jotting down the name and phone number, he handed the sheet to Tiffany.

"Have your lawyer call Ben. He'll give him the facts. The estate hasn't been probated yet. We're still appraising the paintings. But they are not going to bring in a lot of money."

"You're trying to make me believe that, but it won't work. After they go on sale at her gallery, they'll skyrocket in price. And that's when to sell. I'll be there to make sure I get my baby's share!"

She folded the paper and put it in her slim purse and flounced out the front door.

Laura looked after her, wondering what was going to happen next.

"That was...enlightening," Jed said. "Did you know about her?"

"She's the woman to whom the clothing must have belonged,"

Laura said slowly. "I only found out about her the day before Jordan died."

"How?"

She took a breath. "I came by and they were in bed together."

He swore. "You were not expected, I take it."

"No. Jordan said it didn't mean anything. He wanted me to discuss the matter with him, but I said no."

"I see now why you don't want the engagement ring."

"It would mean nothing. Just like it did when he gave it to me. She's four months pregnant, which means they were seeing each other at least a month or longer before he died." She tried to ignore what that did to her. Had Jordan had any regard for her at all?

"I'm sorry," Jed said.

"Yeah, me, too."

"My mother didn't know?"

"I didn't tell anyone. He died so soon after I found out. There wasn't any reason to hurt your parents." Laura bit her lip. "I was afraid I was the reason he crashed."

"Sounds to me like he was loaded to the gills with liquor, that was the reason he crashed."

"Drinking because I broke it off?"

"With Tiffany warming his bed, I doubt it."

Laura nodded, feeling hurt Jed would so quickly dismiss her impact on Jordan's life. "There wasn't much else to say after that." Laura headed for the door.

"I have to get back to the gallery." She almost asked what Jed planned to do about Tiffany, but decided she really didn't want to know. Jordan had made his choices and she'd made hers. The sooner she moved on, the better.

"Laura?"

She stopped at the door and looked back.

"Jordan let the better woman get away," he said.

She knew he was trying to make her feel better. She nodded and walked out.

But she wished for a moment that Jed had said more. Asked her to stay a little longer. She knew he never would. She couldn't believe she'd murmured Jordan's name when he kissed her. She had not been thinking about Jordan except how Jed's kisses were so much more than his brother's. Was there any way to convince him of that?

Heather was in the gallery when Laura returned.

"What are you doing here?" Laura asked.

"Came by to help get the alcove ready. And to check out a rumor. Was there really some woman here who claims to be carrying Jordan's baby?"

"Where did you hear that?"

"At the market. Alice Rose was telling anyone who would listen. She'd gotten it from the guy at the gas station when the woman asked directions. Lots of blond hair and very pretty, according to Alice Rose."

"She's dealing with Jed. He's handling the estate."

"Wish he'd handle my estate," Heather said. "He's yummy."

"He looks like Jordan."

"Ah, but there's a difference. You've noticed. They may look alike, but Jed is a lot steadier. More of a man's man, if you know what I mean."

"Like?"

"He likes women, don't get me wrong, but he's not here to charm our pants off, which I always thought was Jordan's goal in life."

"That's how you see them?"

"Jed is a man confident in his own self-worth. Jordan was narcissistic. And he was always on, if you know what I mean," Heather said.

"I do." At the time it had not bothered Laura. She'd been

thrilled with his attention. But in retrospect, would he have always needed more reassurance than she could have given?

The phone rang as Laura entered her office.

"Hello?" she answered, placing her purse in a desk drawer.

"Laura, my dear. How are you?" It was Maria Brodie.

"I'm well, Maria. How are you?"

"Coping. It's not easy, is it?"

"What can I do for you?" Laura wasn't going to get sucked into Maria's lamenting today. She'd had enough drama.

"Jefferson suggested we have dinner together Thursday evening. It seems like ages since we all got together. And it will give us one last time to discuss the show."

"I don't know," Laura stalled. She did not wish to have dinner at the Brodies.

"I'll have Jed pick you up at seven. We will eat on the patio. He's staying at Jordan's cottage, you know. So helpful to have him packing away Jordan's things. I simply couldn't bear it."

If Jed was going, it would be easier to face the others. "Seven, then."

Was Maria going to ignore Tiffany? Laura didn't know how to bring it up without sounding like she was seeking gossip. After another minute of conversation, she hung up feeling sympathy for Maria. It has to be so hard to lose a child, no matter what the age. And to find him less than perfect would hurt.

Yet Maria did have another son. Maybe she should be a bit more grateful for that son.

Not that it was Laura's place to determine their family dynamics. Today had been too awkward. She couldn't wait to escape the cottage. Did he feel as disconcerted with Tiffany's news? Or didn't men feel the same way?

Jed watched as Laura drove away, then closed the door. What a mess his brother had caused. Had he really asked Laura to marry him as an entry into the gallery scene? Surely he had to know she had too much integrity to try to foist his work on the public at anything above its real value. Anything else wouldn't do her own reputation as an art dealer any good.

But to be seeing another woman while engaged was beyond the pale. How could he do that?

Jed knew. Jordan had gone through life as if it owed him. Nothing stuck. Jed wondered if some of the fault could be directed toward him. Hadn't he been getting his brother out of scrapes since school days? He'd known Jordan was the fair-haired son. He'd done his best to keep Jordan out of trouble, so his parents would find him of some worth, as well.

In retrospect, he'd not done either of them any favors. His parents expected him to rescue Jordan whenever he needed it. And by doing so, he'd never let Jordan learn valuable lessons which would have gone a long way to develop a stronger character.

Maybe his morals would never have been strong, but he might have been more circumspect about the feelings of others.

It made Jed feel almost sick to imagine how Laura must have felt that day, walking in to discover what she did. He wanted to protect her, keep her safe from any hurt. She'd been carrying that burden for months. He'd only just learned about it. If Jordan was around, he'd punch him in the nose.

The phone rang and he went to answer it.

"I've invited Laura to dinner Thursday evening. Would you please pick her up? We need to discuss the showing," his mother said without greeting. "I also want to make it clear to her that we still regard her as family. She almost married your brother, you know."

Jed knew full well that to his mother Laura represented part of the shrine to Jordan's memory. What did she think about Tiffany? He asked.

"Do not speak to me about that…that floozy. She's just trying to cash in on Jordan's fame. I don't for a minute believe she's pregnant, much less with Jordan's child. She's too slim. If she thinks she can extort us into giving her money, she's in for a rude awakening."

"There are DNA tests that can prove or disprove without a doubt," he mentioned.

"Ha, let her try. That is not the purpose of dinner. Please do not bring her name up when Laura is here. This is a family dinner. I want it to go smoothly."

Jed's instincts went on alert. "Family?"

"Your father, me and Jordan's brother with Jordan's fiancée."

So that was it. She was trying to force a role on him different from what she suspected. He could alleviate all her worries by telling her Laura only saw him as a stand-in for Jordan. It was not a role he would take.

"I'll pick her up at seven," he said.

When finished his conversation with his mother, he called the attorney to alert him to the new development. Jed laid out his terms, before any talk was done about the estate, he wanted DNA proof Tiffany's baby was Jordan's. Often physicians would not take samples from in utero fetuses, so they may have to wait until after Tiffany delivered. Jed planned to let the attorney deal with all that. He had enough on his plate.

He leaned back in the chair and looked around the room his brother had used as an office. He'd have to go through all the papers here and put them in some sort of order, tossing what wasn't needed, organizing those that were. Paying any bills still outstanding.

He reached for a box near the desk, surprised to find it heavy. Opening it, Jed saw a stack of papers—all covered with black pen-and-ink drawings. He picked up several and looked at them. The top three were of Tiffany, in various stages of undress. One of Laura looking pensive. A couple of people he didn't recognize. One of his father working on a marble sculpture.

These were excellent. Why had Jordan wasted time on mediocre oil paintings when he could capture nuances and emotions so well in this medium?

Maybe he'd ask. He dialed Laura's gallery. The phone rang and rang. Checking his watch, Jed noted it was after six. She was undoubtedly home. He looked up her phone number and began to dial, when he decided he'd take the pictures to her. She could tell him more about them if she actually saw them.

It was not an excuse to see her.

It sure felt like one.

He didn't care. He wanted to make sure she was doing all right after today's revelations. As Jordan's brother, didn't he have a family responsibility?

Carefully restacking the pictures, he placed them in the box and headed out. All but the ones of Tiffany. He wasn't showing those to anyone.

When he knocked on the door to Laura's flat, he'd second thoughts. He could have waited until morning and taken them into the gallery to ask for a formal appraisal. He could also call Foster again. He'd given Jed a second opinion on the paintings. He'd be a good choice for these.

Laura opened the door. She'd changed into shorts and a cropped top. Her hair was piled up on her head to bare her neck. Her feet were bare. For a moment Jed forgot why he'd come. She looked young and carefree and pretty. He had a hard time remembering she was off-limits.

"Hi, Jed, I didn't expect to see you again today," she said. "Is there a problem?"

"Not exactly. I wanted your opinion on something," he said, holding up the box. "I found these."

"Come in. What's in the box?"

He put it on the dining table and took off the lid.

"Oh, my," she said, reaching for the top drawing.

A pensive pen-and-ink drawing of Laura gazing over the sea was on top. Slowly Laura turned over the papers, one by one, laying them on top of the table as she withdrew them from the box.

"I never saw these," she murmured. "Oh, isn't this great of Peter." She indicated a fisherman at the dock. More and more were picked up.

"These are amazing. I knew he did pen-and-ink. He always had a pad handy, said it kept him in the mood. But I only saw a couple before this. I have the one he gave me. I had no idea he had so many. These are wonderful."

She pulled out a chair and sat, forgetting Jed was even in the room as she happily took one sketch after another. Soon she began sorting them. He sat and watched her, fascinated by the intensity with which she studied each picture. She had not been this excited about the paintings.

"They're good," he said when she reached the bottom of the box.

"Oh, Jed, they're wonderful. Look at the variety. He was especially good at portraitures. You don't know most of the people here, but I do and Jordan captured not only their likeness, but something of their personalities, as well. Why didn't he tell me he was doing these?"

"I have no idea. But there are well over a hundred in this box."

"Did you look for others?" she asked, looking up at him.

"No. Do you think there are more?"

"I don't know. I didn't know about these. But if so, we need to appraise them. These will sell well, I know it. They won't command as much as an oil painting by a proven artist, but they'll sell better than dockside paintings, which is what his oils would go for."

"I need to have them all sell. Things have changed as of today."

"You mean Tiffany?"

"Who else?"

"Are you going to make sure the baby is Jordan's?" she asked.

"I've already talked to the attorney about it. But I don't have any doubts."

Laura looked at the stacks she'd made. "I don't, either. It's so sad. How could he have crashed his car if he was going to become a father?"

"He didn't know. You heard Tiffany," Jed said. "Besides, I doubt if knowing would have changed anything."

"He might have done things differently. He could have married her," Laura said.

Jed shook his head. "I don't believe he would have married Tiffany. Not once mother got a look at her."

"You mother didn't run his life."

"To one extent—she provided the money. He would not risk cutting that off."

"Then he could have gotten a job to support himself," she said with some asperity.

"If he wanted to do that, he would have done so. Tiffany was one of many beautiful blondes he liked to date."

"What happened other times?"

"Nothing important. Dammit, no matter what, our conversations always lead back to Jordan. I feel he's sitting right between us at every instant," Jed said in frustration.

"He's the reason we met," she said.

"For once I'd like to have a conversation without him. Just you and me."

"We have. Contrary to what you think, Jordan is not at the forefront of my mind. He hasn't been since I found him and Tiffany. I did not confuse you two the other night." There, she'd told him again. Please, let him listen.

Jed didn't say anything for a moment, then he pointed to the drawings. "Good enough for the show?"

"Absolutely! Good grief, I'm supposed to give the final okay for the brochure to the printer tomorrow. I need to select which of these I want to show, and write a description and set a price. If you want pricing on all of the ones on display, I'll have to do that, as well. I hope I can get it done before he closes tomorrow. It's cutting it close, but I don't know how else to get it all in. These are too good to leave out. And if your decision to raise money holds, we need to assign a value on the other displayed pieces and see if they will sell."

"Let me help."

She tilted her head slightly looking at him. "Okay. You don't know any of these people so you won't be influenced that way. Pick out the ones you like best as a potential customer. Ones that you might buy if you were in the market."

"That's not very scientific."

"Actually it is. You know what you like. I'll check behind you to see if they really hold potential."

They worked together for more than an hour. It was growing late when they stopped.

"I could do an entire exhibit on the pen-and-ink," she said, taking the dozen they'd selected to show. "Maybe later in the summer, if these sell well, I could do a special," she said. She carefully stacked the pages and put them back in the box. "I can't get to appraising these for a few days."

"No rush, as it turns out. I need to raise as much money from the estate as I can. Tiffany's baby is my niece or nephew."

Laura smiled. "That's right, you'll be the baby's uncle. And your folks will be grandparents. Do you think they'll like that idea when they get used to it?"

"No."

She looked surprised. Jed knew she'd be delighted at the thought of a new baby in the family. Why hadn't Jordan snapped her up when he had the chance? "It'll be competition. One thing about my parents, they are very competitive for attention. You know that, you work with them."

"I see them in a different light as artists. I never thought about how your home life was."

"It was different from my friends', but the only one I knew. They aren't bad parents, just a bit narrow in their focus," Jed said. He accepted long ago his parents were as they were. It saved a lot of tension in the long run. They would never change. He no longer wanted them to.

He rose and pushed in his chair. "I'll leave the box with you. Let me know if you need help when appraising. I'm good at taking notes."

"You're good at a few other things, as well," she murmured, looking up at him. He could read the interest. For a moment he let himself remember how she'd felt in his arms, how her mouth had moved beneath his. How he wished he could sweep her away to some secret place and learn every thing there was to know about her and count the world well lost. But however much he wanted that, it wasn't going to happen.

She still saw him as Jordan. No matter what she said, she was disappointed in his brother, hurt in a deeply personal way by his betrayal. Yet despite it all, she had called for Jordan.

CHAPTER EIGHT

THE next morning Laura woke early. She had trouble sleeping as she realized time was moving swiftly and Jed would be leaving soon. She dressed for the day, then fixed herself a light breakfast. While eating, she began jotting down descriptions for the newly discovered drawings. She was more excited about these than all the other paintings she'd seen. She knew which of the frames she'd use to highlight the stark black-and-white sketches.

Once satisfied, she headed for the gallery to type up the new descriptions on the computer and decide where she would place them on the walls. Maybe grouped together on the back wall of the alcove.

By the time Heather arrived shortly before ten, Laura had the show booklet ready to go except for pricing. She took the draft and walked to the alcove, looking at the pictures, assigning a value that would be used as a start for negotiations. She'd tell Jed he needed to be willing to come down at least ten percent. But hold firm beyond that. Many times patrons offered full price.

She finished assigning prices, labeled how she'd hang the pen-and-ink drawings and gave the entire draft to Heather to take to the printer's. She wanted to get started framing the new pictures as soon as Heather returned. For the first time, she looked forward to the retrospective rather than dreading it.

Laura spent most of the day working on the framing, finishing around four. Satisfied, she hurried to the alcove to hang them. Rearranging the others took longer than she expected and it was closing time before she finished.

"Want me to wait?" Heather asked.

"No, run along. I won't be much longer," she said, hanging another picture in the exact spot that would highlight it the best.

It turned out to be later than she thought when she was finally satisfied. The printer promised to have the booklet back two days before the event. Now all that was needed was to confirm the refreshments by the caterer. She was using Callie's again, and knew the hors d'oeuvres would taste delicious and be presented perfectly.

Heading for home, she swung by the burger stand for a quick meal. To her surprise Jed sat alone at one of the tables on the deck. She bought her dinner and went to join him.

"Mind if I sit here?" she asked.

He looked up and gestured to the empty chair. "Glad for the company."

The deck was half-full with families and couples eating. The sea reflected the setting sun, a blaze of color against the darkening landscape.

"You're eating late," he said.

"Just finished up the display for the show. Got the brochure information off and now only the lighting remains."

"Need help with that?"

"I could use some. I want to do it on Monday, however. The gallery is closed then, so I can fiddle with the lighting without interrupting any browser's enjoyment of the artwork. What did you do today?"

"Finished going through the office. Trashed a lot of papers. Organized the rest and turned them over to the attorney. Fortunately Jordan seemed to have kept up with his bills. Nothing was in arrears and there were no big surprises. I looked for another box of drawings, but didn't find one in the house, but there was one in the garage. I think they're older. Some of the pages are yellowed as if with age."

"Are they as good as the ones I saw?" she asked.

"I think so. If I'd known I was going to see you tonight, I'd have brought them with me. I can drop them off tomorrow if you like."

Laura did not want to talk about Jordan. Here was a perfect chance to show Jed she was not confusing him with his brother. She liked talking with him. Liked him period!

"Or I can run by and pick them up tomorrow afternoon."

"I'm leaving for a few days in Boston," Jed said. "Checking in with the office and then visiting a couple of old friends. I'll be back by next Thursday. The infamous Brodie family dinner, you know."

She nodded, feeling let down.

Jordan's show began on Friday and would run for at least a week.

"I'm glad you're staying longer than originally planned," she said. "I hear the weather is supposed to stay beautiful for another week." Great, she was resorting to banalities.

"As long as it doesn't have rain it's good in my book these days. We get daily showers in the Amazon Basin," he said.

They talked a little longer about the vagaries of the weather. Jed finished before Laura, but stayed to keep her company. She hoped for an invitation to go for a drink or something, but as soon as she finished, he rose and took both plates to the nearby trash.

"If you're leaving in the morning, maybe I should run by tonight and get that other box. Save you time tomorrow," she said. It was still light out, early enough to stop by without making it seem like a big deal.

"Fine. I'll follow you there," he said.

Laura took a second once in her car to run a brush through her hair and recolor her lips. She looked a little tired from lack of sleep, not that Jed noticed.

"Come in, it won't take me a second to get the box," Jed said, throwing open the door when they reached the cottage.

"I'm in no hurry," Laura said, walking into the living room. It no longer looked like the same place she'd visited during her engagement. The curtains were wide-open, as were the windows. The evening breeze swept through, giving a crisp freshness to the room. A briefcase lay opened on the coffee table, stacks of reports, photographs and even a small rolled cylinder of paper rested beside several pens and pencils, paperweights holding them on the table.

She walked over while Jed went to the back of the cottage. The printouts were of spreadsheets with columns of numbers. What caught her attention was the top photograph. It was of a bridge, or a portion of one. She sat on the sofa and picked up the stack. Shuffling through them, she could see each stage captured as building progressed—the pouring of foundations; the initial steel beams jutting from the shore. As she moved through them, she didn't need the dates at the corner of each one to see the progression.

Soaring against the deep blue sky, with thick green foliage surrounding the site, the structure was a study in contrasts. The bridge looked mammoth from snapshots taken close up. But from the distance on the river it looked almost lacy—and beautiful.

"Here is the other box," Jed said, coming back into the living room.

"These are amazing," she said, holding up the photographs. "I kept them in order. These are of the bridge you're building, aren't they?"

"Yes. I usually take pictures as we go. A chronology of events, so to speak."

"It's a lovely structure. This one must have been taken just before you left," she said, holding out one showing almost half the span. The date was four days before she'd first met him.

Jed put down the box and sat next to her. "It was. I brought it home in case my folks wanted to see it."

Laura would bet the gallery they hadn't even asked.

"Tell me about them," she said, holding out the photographs and sitting back on the sofa.

Jed took them and began a brief description of the different stages they'd already completed. He made the site come alive and she soon had a better appreciation of how dangerous the work was, how frustrating dealing with red tape and bureaucratic delays. She gained a new appreciation for the man who patiently fought through all the snafus to get the bridge built. When he unrolled some of the plans she could see how the finished bridge would look.

"Take a picture with the sun glinting on it and the sky so blue. It'd make a terrific study. I could sell it," she said, already envisioning the finished photograph, matted with a silver frame. She didn't carry photographs in her gallery, but had several friends who did. She already had a buyer for Jed's picture of the finished bridge—herself. Besides the beauty it would give, it would be a tie to a man she was finding more and more fascinating.

When he wound down, he glanced out the window, surprised to see the darkness. Checking his watch, he shook his head.

"I talked your ear off. It's after ten."

"The time flew by. I can't believe how dangerously you live. Beyond the basics of falling off the structure, or getting hit in the head by a swinging steel girder, there's disease, lack of hygiene and nutritious foods, insects, snakes." Laura shivered thinking about how many ways Jed could be injured or become ill.

"Sounds worse than it is. And I'm healthy and careful. We all are on the site. There were fewer than twenty injuries last year. Since we have so many unskilled laborers working for us, and a language barrier, that's pretty remarkable."

Laura thought Jed was pretty remarkable, but knew he'd not want to hear that.

She rose and picked up the box of Jordan's sketches, hugging them to her. "Thanks for taking the time to explain so much. I really enjoyed hearing about the bridge. Does it have a name?"

"Not so far. We call it project J-173." He rose and stood near her.

Laura felt her senses go on alert. They were so close.

"I'll walk you out to your car," he said.

The night was black, few lights around. The cottages farther along the road were dark. The air was still warm, though the breeze cooled it down from the heat of the day.

He stopped by the car and Laura turned, leaning against the car for a moment, the box still in her arms. "I enjoyed tonight, Jed," she said.

"I did, too. It's not often I get to discuss my work."

"Too bad, you'd make a great lecturer. Maybe you should give travelogue talks between jobs, showing pictures of the work, and some of the local settings."

He half laughed. "I'm not that interesting, merely an engineer who loves his work."

"And takes justifiable pride in it."

He didn't respond right away. The silence grew.

"Laura," he said softly.

She held her breath until he leaned over to kiss her.

Laura felt the magic of his touch as she had before. She wished she could drop the box of sketches and throw her arms around him. But she dared not do that. Jed threaded his fingers through her hair, his palms cradling her cheeks. He took his time kissing her. Laura felt she was floating. Blood pounded in her veins, her skin felt too tight. She wanted more, to feel his body against hers. To explore, touch, learn.

After endless moments of sheer delight, he pulled back giving light kisses along her jaw, across her cheeks.

"You are so sweet," he said softly.

Finally he stood, releasing her and reaching to open the car door.

"Drive safely home," he said.

She couldn't speak, only nod. Tossing the box onto the seat, she almost reached out for another kiss, but thought better of it. She didn't want anything to mar this special moment and she was afraid if she pushed for more, he'd back off.

As he watched her car drive away, Jed called himself every kind of fool there was. He'd been tempted beyond his ability to resist kissing her. He was lucky to hold on to the belief she liked kissing him. At least this time she hadn't called him by his brother's name.

There was no future here. He had a bridge site to return to and another one on the horizon when this one was completed. His mother believed his interest in Laura was a carryover from the rivalry of their younger days. Who knew what Laura believed? He was not about to ask her.

Turning for the cottage, Jed was glad he'd be leaving tomorrow. Being in Boston would give him some distance to gain perspective. When he returned and went to the family dinner, he'd be able to play the part of Jordan's brother. And keep any interest in Laura a secret. He entered and saw the photographs and construction drawings spread across the table. She had been interested, he'd recognized that. A novelty after so many artistic types, he bet.

Slowly he gathered everything up and replaced them in his briefcase. Maybe he'd look up an old girlfriend in Boston and take her out to dinner. Anything to get beyond the idea of becoming involved with Laura Parkerson.

At six fifty-five on Thursday, Laura was pacing her flat. Jed was supposed to pick her up any minute. She had not spoken with him since leaving his cottage the other evening. She was surprised how anxious she was to see him again. She'd done nothing but think about that kiss in the days since. Every time he touched her, she felt a tingle of electricity. His kisses were sensual heaven. She wondered what it would be like to make love with him.

The thought should have shocked her, but more and more over the last few days, she'd dreamed of making love with Jed. Slow and sensuous, with the sound of the surf in the background. The fantasy had kept her awake long into the nights.

Had he gotten past her faux pas of calling him his brother's name? More and more Laura was having trouble remembering Jordan. He seemed like a person she'd known long ago. And not well.

Jed filled her thoughts these days.

The knock on the door came right at seven. Another thing she liked about the man. He was punctual. As a businessperson, she appreciated that.

"Hello," she said, her heart fluttering when she saw him. He looked terrific in the casual shirt and neatly pressed khakis.

"Ready?" His eyes lit in appreciation, but he said nothing.

Disappointed, she nodded, picking up the plate of cookies she'd prepared for the Brodies. "I made some snicker doodles. I hope your parents will like them."

"If they don't I sure do. Maybe I should hope they don't. You'd then have to give them to me," he teased lightly as they walked to his rental car.

"I'm happy to make you a batch all for yourself," she responded. "How was Boston?"

"Great as always. Saw some friends. Did some work at the office there. Our headquarters are in New York, but we have offices in several major cities. Is everything set for the opening of the show tomorrow?"

"Yes. The booklets arrived the day before yesterday, a day early. They came out perfect. I hope you and your parents will be pleased."

She'd been startled when she'd received the finished version and looked at the picture she'd chosen of Jordan to grace the front. It looked so much like Jed, she felt confused. The same smile, same twinkle in his eyes when amused. But she could see the differences, as well. Jordan's jaw was not as strong as Jed's. His face still looked boyish while Jed's was definitely all man. He'd matured, Jordan was forever young.

Laura had been to the Brodie's home several times, first as a representative of the gallery and then as Jordan's fiancée. The last time had been shortly after the funeral when she and Maria planned the retrospective.

The house looked much the same, except the yard and garden seemed neglected. Of course it was high summer, everything looked a tad wilted with the heat. Still, Laura was surprised to see it in slight decay.

Maria threw wide the door when they walked up the path.

"Oh, Laura, it's been too long. You know you are to treat this as your home," she said, gathering her in a warm embrace. "Come in. Jed, thanks for picking her up."

"Some cookies," Laura said, handing Maria the platter.

"Aren't you sweet. You know how much Jefferson and I love cookies." Maria took the platter and escorted them inside the house.

Laura noticed Maria didn't extend the same hug to Jed. Why not? she wondered.

Jefferson was in the living room. He rose when they entered.

"Good to see you again, Laura. Jed, how was Boston?"

"What would everyone like to drink?" Maria asked. "Jed, how long were you in Boston? Did you date any pretty girls while you were there? You need to date when you can. Being in the wilds of Brazil certainly gives you no chance to see women."

Laura looked at Maria, then at Jed. She noticed the slight tightening of his jaw at his mother's comment.

"As a matter of fact, I took Susan Waters out for dinner one night. Remember her from our college days?" he asked, avoiding Laura's gaze.

She looked away quickly. He'd taken someone else out for dinner. Fine. They had no understanding between them. But the dart of jealousy surprised her. She was not getting interested that way in Jordan's brother! She was not!

Except that extraordinary kiss she couldn't forget. Had he kissed Susan Waters like that? Laura frowned, not wanting to picture that scenario. She felt suddenly awkward—like an unwanted fifth wheel.

"How nice. You should invite her out for a visit. Now, while Jefferson gets the drinks, you come with me, Laura. I've finished my tribute to Jordan and want you to see it. If you like it, I want you to show it at the gallery," Maria said, taking Laura's arm gently and leading her toward the studio.

Laura followed Maria from the house to one of two studios that had been built in the backyard. Jefferson's was larger, with a roll-up door that enabled large slabs of stone to be brought in for his sculpting. Maria's studio was comprised of mostly windows, with an expanse on the north wall that was all double-pane glass.

Jed went with them, though Laura had thought he would stay to talk with his father.

Maria dramatically threw open the door and gestured to the large canvas on an easel that faced them.

Laura stepped inside and went to study the painting. It was beautiful, haunting and sad. Maria had captured a garden with weeping flowers, a weeping willow tree to the left. In the right lower corner a figure with white hair, bent over as if in inconsolable grief. A discarded teddy bear lay on the grass at her feet. The colors were vibrant and compelling. At first glance it was a beautiful garden in full blossoms and colors. Closer inspection showed all the flowers drooping slightly, as if in sadness. Everything was slightly blurred, as if seen through tears.

The overall feeling was one of grief and despair. Yet the colors were vibrant, the entire scene reminiscent of the impressionists. How had she managed that? It was what made her one of America's leading painters. Collectors would be thrilled with this latest work.

"Are you really going to sell it?" Laura asked. "It's beautiful. Maybe one of your very best," she said, feasting on the nuances she picked up the longer she studied it.

"It was cathartic. I needed to expunge my deepest grief. But I do not want to see it again. It was enough to do," Maria said, looking out the window.

Laura knew it would bring top dollar, but she herself would not want such a sad painting in her home. Maybe because she knew exactly what caused the painting.

"It's beautiful, Mother," Jed said. "Jordan would have loved it."

"I hope so," she said sadly. "It's my tribute to my precious son."

Dinner was served on the patio, sheltered from the evening breeze. Maria had prepared a ham and potatoes and cabbage meal, served with both red wine and iced tea.

"It was Jordan's favorite," Maria said as she served Laura's plate.

Laura remembered. Every time she'd eaten at the Brodies with Jordan, Maria had served the same meal.

She glanced at Jed suspecting this was not his favorite meal. Had his parents served that his first night home?

"What is your favorite?" she asked him.

"New England clam chowder, lobster and crusty bread," Jefferson said unexpectedly.

Jed looked at his father in surprise. "I didn't know you'd remember."

Jefferson returned his son's look and nodded. Glancing at Maria, he commented, "We will have that one night before you leave."

"Chowder is so hard to prepare," Maria said as she began to eat. "It's difficult to keep the milk from curdling."

"No more difficult than any other meal you prepare, my dear," Jefferson said. "I wouldn't mind some fresh lobster myself. It's been a long time since we've had any. Why live here if we don't take advantage?"

"We live here for more than food," Maria said with some asperity. "I'm sure Jed is glad for any home-cooked meal, working in such outlandish places as he does."

"Speaking of that," Laura said. "Have you seen the pictures he brought home of the bridge they're building? It's really amazing."

Maria and Jefferson looked at her with puzzlement.

"What pictures?" Jefferson asked.

"The ones he takes of the construction, each stage. Jed's done that for each job he's worked on," Laura said, looking at him for confirmation.

He nodded, glancing at his parents.

"Why?" Maria asked.

"To document the different processes and steps in the building. And to capture the feeling of the place where they're being built. The photographs I saw the other evening really gave me a feeling for the challenge of the job. It's not as if they're in downtown Boston with everything close as hand. They are hundreds of miles up the Amazon River with each item, tool, food, everything having to be brought up on barge or boat. Or along the dirt road that the bridge will connect."

Jefferson smiled slightly as he listened to Laura. "Indeed?"

"Many of the men working there are thousands of miles from home. The only communications they have is via computer—when the generators are running to provide electricity, and if the wireless feature is working. Then they're gone for months at a time. In dangerous circumstances, hot weather, no amenities that we take for granted." Laura wanted his parents to understand.

Maria looked perplexed. "Is that true, Jed?"

"Pretty much," he said.

"I had no idea." She looked at her son as if he were an alien species.

"You would if you asked him about his job," Laura said with annoyance. These people had a wonderful man for a son and seemed to completely ignore him.

"I've never quite understood why anyone would do such a thing," Maria said.

"I enjoy building," Jed said. He looked amused when he met Laura's gaze. "And I've never had such an ardent advocate before."

"You've accomplished a lot. And it will last long after you have gone," she said.

"Like a granite sculpture," Jefferson said.

"Only Jed sculpts with steel," Laura murmured.

"You make it sound artistic. It's just a bridge," Maria said.

"You should see it, it's beautiful, or will be when finished. I've asked for photographs."

"Whatever for?" the older woman asked.

"To sell, of course. I don't normally sell photographs, but in this case will make an exception." She had not known she was going to say that. From the startled look on all three faces, no one else had expected that, either. But, darn it, she wanted Jed to get some interest or respect or something from his family. Didn't they realize what a special man he was? What he was doing was important!

"I can't believe I'm hearing you say that, Laura," Maria said. "After all the times Jordan tried to get you to exhibit his work and you refused. Now you're talking about showing a bunch of pictures? *Of a construction site?*"

Laura fell silent. She couldn't argue that point. More than once in public Jordan had tried to cajole her into giving him the showing he wanted. They had fought over that issue several times. At the time, she'd pleaded with him to stop asking, but he seemed to think causing a confrontation in public would have her give in more easily. He'd learned that would not work.

"There's a difference," she said at last.

"And that being?" Maria was not willing to give her the benefit of the doubt, Laura knew that.

"Photographs would be quite different," Jed said, breaking into the tension. "Jordan would have needed to compete with artists of your caliber for a showing at her gallery. Any pictures she chose to show would have little or no competition, and would be solely for the novelty aspect."

"It's not art," Maria said.

"I think there would be a market for it," Laura said. "Not the same collectors who buy your paintings, but there are lots of people who prefer photographs to paintings. It's not a market I've branched into, but I might. If Jed delivers the pictures."

"Jed is not an artist. Not like Jordan was."

"Maria," Laura said gently. "You need to come see the paintings before the opening tomorrow night."

"It's going to be hard enough to be there at all. I need the fortification of friends and neighbors."

"Is there a problem?" Jefferson asked. "This is not the first time you've tried to get us to see the paintings."

"I think you'll both be disappointed. Jordan wasn't up to Maria's caliber," she said diplomatically.

"He had talent. Once the retrospective has been reviewed, appreciation for his work will grow. He had such potential. I can't bear to think it's gone forever."

"He didn't live up to what promise he showed as a kid, Mother," Jed said gently.

"How dare you denigrate your brother's work! You are nothing but an engineer, what do you know about art? You were jealous of Jordan as children, as teenagers and still are, as far as I can tell. Are you making cozy with Laura trying to win her over—take her away from your brother? It won't work, she'll see through you in an instant! She loved Jordan. He was an artist. She runs an art gallery. It was a perfect match."

"Jordan is dead. Even if I wanted to take anything of his, what would it matter? He'd never know."

"But you'd believe you finally beat him out. Would that make you feel like the better man?" Maria was getting carried away.

Laura wanted to say Jed didn't need to do anything to be the better man, but wisely kept quiet. The evening was fast getting out of hand and she didn't want to do anything to make it worse.

"Be warned, Laura, Jed and Jordan had a fierce rivalry all their lives. He may seem interested in you now, but it's only because Jordan was," Maria said spitefully.

"As children maybe they were competitive, but I hardly think they would be so now. As far as I can tell, Jed hasn't been around for the last decade. Hardly conducive to continued rivalry," Laura said, trying to interject some calmness into the conversation.

"He was always jealous of his brother," Maria said.

"Hardly fair, Maria," Jefferson said. "As children they were in and out of scrapes, but Jed has not competed with his brother in any way over the last decade. They couldn't be more dissimilar despite being twins. And from where I'm sitting, Jed has far more to be jealous of than Jordan did. He's made a success in a very competitive field. Remarkable in and of itself, but he did without any help from us. He hasn't asked us for a dime since he began his junior year in college."

The statement needed no further explanation. Jordan had been subsidized by his mother and everyone there knew it.

CHAPTER NINE

LAURA began to count the seconds until she could escape. She marveled that Jed could keep his calm demeanor and talk easily with his father after his mother's scathing comments. If she ever had children, Laura vowed, she'd never play favorites.

At last the lengthy meal ended.

"I have to get home. I need to be up early tomorrow to put the finishing touches on the exhibit. We close at six as normal and then we reopen at seven o'clock for the reception. I'd love you to see the paintings before the general public, Maria." Laura had to try once more. "If only to see if I've priced them competitively."

Maria raised an eyebrow. "Priced them. I said they weren't for sale."

Laura took a deep breath and looked at Jed for guidance. He came to her rescue.

"I told her to price them and sell them if she can. Circumstances have changed in the last few days. The estate may need as much money as it can bring in."

"I said they weren't for sale."

"You can buy them if you want to keep them, Mom. It's not as if some of the money wouldn't be distributed back to you," Jed said.

"It's the principle of the thing," she said. "He was my son. His work should stay in the family."

"He was our son and you've often said he needed to get his work out into the world so people would appreciate his talent," Jefferson said. "Let's see what happens."

Laura met Jed's gaze. They knew the world would never appreciate the work as Maria imagined.

"Thank you for dinner, Mom. Dad, it was good to talk with you," Jed said, rising. He wasn't one to mess around. It was past time to leave. Laura added her thanks and quickly got up to follow him.

Once in the car, backing from the driveway, Laura turned to him.

"Are your family dinners always this exciting?"

"This was mellow. My mother hasn't quite grasped the meaning of tact."

Laura felt suddenly grateful for the love in her own family. Her parents didn't understand her desire to live by the sea, but they supported her in every way they could. She always knew she was loved for being herself.

"Thanks for coming to bat for me," Jed said. "Novel experience. I can't remember when someone stood up for me before. Except once in college."

"What happened then?"

"Not much, a case of mistaken identity. A friend vouched for me and the matter was closed."

She knew there was more to the story, but if he didn't want to share it with her, she wouldn't push. Their relationship was too fragile to stand up to any demands. If they had a relationship. Maria certainly had done her best to nip any inclinations that way in the bud. And what about that woman he'd seen in Boston?

Her optimism dimmed. Jed had never given her any hint of a future. He had said how much he loved his job. And she didn't have the kind of career that would allow her to pack up to follow him to the remote outreaches of the world.

"Anything I can do to help with the exhibit tomorrow?" Jed asked.

"Just lend moral support when I open the doors at seven," she said. She was growing more and more nervous as the time approached. She wanted the showing to go well, but knew she couldn't count on anything. Patrons of the arts were sometimes fickle. They could make or break an exhibit with the most curious reasons.

"I'll be leaving the end of next week. By then we'll have an idea of how the sales will go. I have my appraisals for tax purposes. Any that sell for more, I'll just pay the extra tax. Would you take me sailing once more before I leave?"

Laura looked at him in surprise. She smiled. "How about Monday? It's a free day for me with the gallery closed. And I think I'll be ready for some serious escape," she said, hoping she hid the disappointment that swept through her when he gave his departure date. She wondered if she was up to anything special developing between them.

She was afraid to trust her own feelings in the matter, having so recently been burned by his brother. Were they more alike than she wanted to believe? Was there any truth to Maria's accusations that if Jed tried to make a play it was to one-up his brother? She didn't think Jed played games like that. But on the day she got engaged, she'd have said the same thing about Jordan.

At six forty-five the next evening, Laura unlocked the doors to the gallery. She and Heather both wore black cocktail dresses. Callie had set up the hors d'oeuvres and wine at a spot near the sales counter. She and another woman would staff it during the evening, keeping everything replenished.

The lighting had come off perfect, highlighting the pictures and drawings to perfection. Laura especially liked how the pen-and-ink drawings looked so dramatic—their stark lines such a contrast from the colorful paintings.

"If no one comes, we'll have enough food to last us for a month," she commented to Heather as she straightened the spread of brochures on a small table near the door. Jordan's face smiled up at her. Laura tried once again to see the differences between the two brothers. Jordan lacked the steadiness Jed evidenced. She could depend on Jed. If she could get beyond Jordan's betrayal. It wasn't fair to tar Jed with the same brush, just because he looked like his brother.

And because he'd seen that woman in Boston.

"At least he was up-front about it," she said softly.

"What?" Heather asked.

"Nothing." Would he have said anything if his mother hadn't asked?

"Here comes the first customer. Oh, it's Jed. I don't guess he'll be buying anything." Heather gave him a wide smile.

Jed had dressed in his business suit for the evening. The snowy-white shirt contrasted with his deep tan. His blue eyes seemed to smile when he spotted Laura.

Casting a curious glance around the gallery, he absorbed everything as he walked over to her.

"It looks terrific. Better than I expected, given what you had to work with."

"There speaks a son of a famous painter. I bet most of the tourists who stop by over the next week will love some of these seascapes," Heather said.

"We're hoping for that, anyway. And the publicity of his being a local artist," Laura said. She hoped someone would buy one painting. Just one.

The chimes at the door sounded as a couple hesitantly entered.

"I think I'll prop open the door. I don't want there to be any question we are open for business," Laura said.

By seven-thirty the gallery was full of both locals and tourists. Other gallery owners had stopped by to offer support and see what the work of Maria Brodie's son was like. The remarks were kind, but bland. Except for the pen-and-ink drawings. They brought the most excitement to the event.

"Oh, oh, trouble at six o'clock," Jed said softly to Laura. They had just walked away from talking with the mayor when Jed glanced over her shoulder.

Laura turned and saw Tiffany walk into the place as if she were on a mission. She wore skintight black pants and a fuchsia top that hugged her generous endowments. She headed directly to the alcove, scooping up a brochure on her way.

"She has as much right as anyone else to be here. I just hope she doesn't cause trouble," Laura said. There was no way anyone was going to ignore her. Her hair cascaded halfway down her back. She walked as though she was on a model's runway. Her makeup would keep the cosmetic business in the black for a year. She so didn't look as if she belonged in the gallery.

Jed gave her a disbelieving look. "Honey, women like Tiffany are trouble. They don't just cause it."

Laura watched her for a moment, but she seemed to be doing little more than checking the pricing and noting them on the catalog. There was an order form in the back with the prices listed, but Laura didn't feel the need to inform the woman. Let her figure it out for herself. She was not high on Laura's list of favorite people.

She couldn't help remembering the shock of finding this woman in bed with her fiancé. The disbelief that she stood casually wrapped in a sheet and witnessed the scene between Jordan and herself. He could have at least had the decency to tell her to get lost while they were breaking up.

Just then there was an increase in the noise level and she turned, seeing Maria and Jefferson enter like royalty. Locals went to greet them, whether they knew them or not. Both were famous residents and that was enough.

Laura moved through the crowd to greet them. Magically

the group around them parted, allowing them a clear path to the alcove.

Maria walked stoically to the exhibit. Her eyes swept the display. She gasped. "What have you done?" she hissed, staring at the paintings.

Moving closer she looked at the left wall. A half dozen seascapes mingled with some garden studies. She examined each painting, exclaiming with outrage. Moving to the back wall, she let out a low groan.

"How dare you put up sketches! This was not what Jordan was about. He was a gifted painter. Where are his masterpieces? You have ruined everything. I demand you get his better works out here immediately. How dare you make a mockery of all he stood for!"

She turned and saw Tiffany. She glared at her. "What are you doing here?"

"I came to see Jordan's paintings," the woman said. "I have every right to be here, maybe more than most. Jordan talked a good line, but he obviously had an inflated opinion of his worth."

Maria turned to Laura. "Is this some kind of retribution for an imagined betrayal because of this floozy? Where are the good paintings? How dare you malign Jordan's memory this way! I trusted you. You of all people should have done your best by him. He loved you. You were to be married. How can you call yourself a respectable gallery dealer when you play such a rotten trick behind my back?"

The crowd fell silent as Maria's voice rose.

"These are his good paintings," Laura said quietly, excruciatingly aware of the silence around them. Every eye was trained on Maria. "I suspected they were not of the caliber you expected. But they are the best I found. This is why I asked you repeatedly to come see them first. Maria, this is his best work."

"*Liar!* He had a portfolio from years of work. I should have selected the paintings myself. It was too painful, but this is beyond anything. You have besmirched his good name. How dare you! Take these down immediately. I will not have them up for people to think of as Jordan's work. And I'll see to it that no respectable artist ever deals with you again!"

The crowd seemed to move closer, so not to miss a single nuance of the scene unfolding.

"That's enough, Mother," Jed said, stepping in to grasp her arm. He gently led her through the crowd.

"Do not take that woman's side in this. She's ruined your brother's reputation. How dare she put up such amateurish paintings! It's to get back at the family because of that woman's allegations she's carrying Jordan's child. It's a lie. How could Laura ever believe such a thing? She was engaged to him! Jordan loved her."

Jed didn't say anything, but relentlessly drew his mother into the privacy of the workshop in the back. Laura almost ran to catch up with them, Jefferson right beside her.

Once inside, Laura wanted to sink through the floor. What must everyone think? It seemed as if a good third of the town was present. They would have heard every word. Would they think that she had deliberately put up poor quality work? What would this do to her gallery's reputation?

She pushed the door, but before it closed, Tiffany walked in. She was the one who slammed the door.

"If you want proof this baby is Jordan's, I'll have it soon. My doctor agreed to do the DNA testing," she said.

Laura knew the evening just got worse.

Maria glared at her. "You slut. Stay away from my family. Jefferson, get rid of her."

"Now, my dear, let's hear what she has to say. If DNA testing shows she's carrying our son's baby, maybe we misjudged things." He looked at Tiffany expectantly.

"Never. Jordan was engaged to Laura," Maria said, glaring at Tiffany.

"Until I found him in bed with Tiffany," Laura said. If the damage Maria had done stuck, she could be looking to open a gallery in a new town before long.

"What?" Maria looked stunned. "That's not true!"

"Unfortunately it is," Laura said. "Not a happy memory for me. I thought he really loved me."

"He wanted her to sell his paintings. He wanted to make his mark on the world and take me with him when he moved on. We were going to Paris once he got some money of his own," Tiffany said. "Now he's gone. God, what a waste. He was so special. And he loved me!"

"What about Laura?" Jefferson asked bewildered.

Tiffany shrugged. "She never told him she wanted to go to Paris."

"They were engaged."

"He had second thoughts after he met me."

"Or all along. I think he hoped I'd be the ticket for some sales. But, Maria, you've seen his best work. Honestly, I selected the ones I thought showed best. Of everything I've seen, and Jed and I went through everything, his pen-and-ink sketches turn out to be the most unique and marketable. They won't ever rival what you earn for your work, but ought to bring in a respectable amount—especially if there's controlled selling, so we don't flood the market."

"Enough to start a college fund for Jordan's child," Jed said.

Maria drew in a deep breath. "He cannot have fathered a child with that woman."

"Sure he could have. Most likely did," Jed said, grimly. "It's just like him. Only this time I wasn't around to take the fall."

"That was a misunderstanding," Maria snapped.

"What was?" Tiffany asked, wide-eyed.

"It's of no concern to you," Maria said. "Get out."

Tiffany frowned at her. "I'm leaving. Too much drama. But my attorney has already talked to Jordan's and before long you'll have to acknowledge I'm carrying his child. I want my share for my baby."

"We will do what's right," Jed said, ignoring his mother's groan of protest.

"Okay, then," Tiffany said. She turned and opened the door and made a grand exit.

No one spoke for a long moment.

"You know, if she is carrying Jordan's child, that baby will be your first grandchild," Laura said slowly. "A part of Jordan living on."

Maria turned her gaze to Laura. She didn't move for a moment, then her eyes filled with tears. "Was that really his best work?"

Laura nodded.

"You should have gone over the paintings and chosen the ones you liked, Mom," Jed said gently. "Or decided not to submit them to the general public view."

"They are so amateurish," she said, perplexed. "He had such potential as a child. Such promise."

"But no drive to develop it," Jed said. "You know he liked the easy way out."

"And we made it even easier by funding his lifestyle. Maybe if he'd had a few setbacks like we overcame at the beginning, he would have tried harder," Jefferson said slowly. He looked sadly at his wife.

"It was because we had it so hard at first I wanted things to be easier for him," she said.

"People gain strength from adversity," Laura said.

Maria went to Jefferson. "Take me home, please." As they walked to the door, she looked at Laura. "Take everything down and get rid of it all. I do not want the entire town laughing at Jordan."

"They aren't laughing, Maria. The work shows what Miragansett is famous for, our beaches and seascapes. There will be people who will enjoy looking at the paintings, not caring whether they are stellar work or not or by some famous artist. The images will bring them pleasure." Laura's heart ached for the defeated woman. She'd come to terms with Jordan a month or two ago. Maria had to face up to facts now.

Maria just shook her head. "My precious son."

"You have another," Laura said, angry the woman couldn't seem to see beyond her image of one son to the reality of another.

Jefferson looked at Jed. "We do indeed. And a fine man, one I'm proud of."

Jed inclined his head slightly. "Thanks, Dad."

Maria leaned against Jefferson and didn't say a word.

When they had left, Laura leaned against one of the worktables. "I hate to go back out there," she said, looking at the closed door separating them from the gallery.

"Adversity strengthens you," he murmured. Holding out his hand, he waited.

She put hers into it.

"I hate it when people quote my own words back at me."

He laughed. "You're strong enough. You and your gallery will survive this. Most people will see it as merely an acknowledgment of a man who died young. Sentimentality never hurt artistic sales, you know."

Feeling better about everything with Jed's hand wrapped around hers, she moved to the door. It wasn't fair to leave Heather in the lurch.

Head held high, Laura stepped into the gallery. The level of conversation had resumed to its earlier level. It didn't appear as if the crowd had diminished at all. She looked for Heather, surprised to see her behind the counter, a line of people clearly waiting to be served.

Her friend Sally came up from behind her.

"Laura, this is fantastic! I hear everyone is hurrying to buy something because Maria Brodie told you not to sell anything. Is that true?"

"She said it, but she's not the one in charge," Jed said, stepping beside Laura and looking at Sally.

"Sally, this is Jed Brodie."

"I figured that out myself when I saw him. Sally Benson. I knew you were twins, but you could be Jordan standing here. I'm sure you've heard that a million times."

He inclined his head, his gaze then scanning the room and the line at the counter.

"Do we tell them the paintings will remain available?" Laura asked doubtfully.

"Are you nuts? This is the best thing to happen," Sally said. "No need to worry about the reputation of your gallery now, Laura. It'll be forever known as a happening place. I'm just sorry I got here too late for the big scene. I can't believe Tiffany showed up."

"You know her?" Jed asked.

Sally shook her head. "Only what I heard from Laura. I didn't know Jordan did pen-and-ink drawings. They're really good. If he did some of the cove, I might be interested in one myself."

"I knew he sketched sometimes, but I had no idea of the number of pieces he had done. I expect Jed will be able to sell them a few at a time for years to come. And their value will only increase since no more will be forthcoming," Laura said, breathing a little more easily that the mood of the event seemed to have moved to upbeat and positive.

"I'm going to mingle and scoop up any gossip I can," Sally said with a wide smile. She sauntered back toward the alcove, stopping to speak to a couple she knew.

"It seems a long time until nine," Laura said, glancing at her watch. "I'll go help Heather."

Jed tried to stay in the background, but once alone, it was as if he were fair game. Men and women who had known Jordan came over to talk to him. Many asked if he, too, was artistic.

They seemed surprised when he told them he was an engineer. More than one woman flirted. He wasn't surprised. People often confused him and Jordan when his brother had been alive. For the first time since arriving, he couldn't wait to return to the Amazon. At least there he knew what to expect.

By nine, he was happier than Laura to close the gallery. There were people lingering, still talking, eating the delicious hors d'oeuvres and getting one last glass of wine. He wanted to suggest they take it with them, but knew that wouldn't go over big. He looked for Laura, seeing her with a customer, laughing at something the woman had said. How she could still look fresh and happy was beyond him. He knew she'd had a long day. Had the dramatic scene with his mother proved too much? Would she even want to have him take her home?

Finally the last of the guests left. Laura closed the door and pulled the shade, leaning against the wooden frame.

"I'm beat!" she said.

"Me, too," Callie said, as she and her assistant began to competently package up the leftover food. "Want this now, or shall I freeze it?" she asked.

"Give me and Heather enough for a couple of days now and freeze the rest. Thanks again, Callie, it was lovely."

"I'll say," Heather said, coming from behind the counter and kicking off her shoes. "If I hadn't been so busy, I'd have eaten more, but I had my hands full. We sold everything and have several wanting to see what else is available. I have a list." She grabbed a couple of crab puffs before Callie wrapped them up.

"Fantastic. Let's deliver all the sold items and showcase other paintings and see if we can sell those, as well," Laura said, pushing away and walking to the alcove. "Several of the people bought the frames the paintings are in, so I'll need to get some replacements. Same with the pen-and-ink frames. I think I'll plan to sell those in the frames from now on." She walked around the display, already deep in thought. Jed wondered if she remembered the rest of them were there.

"Come by tomorrow and we'll pick out some more. Or I can bring all I have here and you can sell them as you can. Unless you don't have the room," he said.

She turned and frowned.

"That would put me short on space, but when you leave, I'll need access. Let me rearrange some things in back and see if we can squeeze them in."

Jed waited until Laura was ready to leave before departing. "I want to take you home. It's late."

"My car is here. I wasn't planning to walk home this late."

"It'll be safe here overnight."

She nodded. Bidding Heather good-night, Laura locked up and went with Jed to his rental car.

"Are you holding up all right?" he asked as he drove the short distance to her flat.

She nodded. Truth be told, she was more worried about Jed and his relationship with his parents than the situation with Jordan. She'd had several months to get over the initial hurt and betrayal. But Jed and Maria and Jefferson had only learned the facts recently.

He walked her up to her flat, stopping at the door. Taking her key he unlocked it for her.

"Did you want to come in?" she asked breathlessly.

"Not tonight. I'll have the paintings ready to go in the morning. Take care of yourself," he said, brushing his lips lightly over hers.

Turning to leave, Jed regretted not staying. But Laura was tired. Plus, he didn't want sympathy tonight. If she was only feeling sorry for the family because of the revelations from Tiffany, he'd just as soon not know that. He was not after his brother's fiancée, but now that he knew Laura had ended that relationship before his death, weren't all bets off? She was not Jordan's fiancée. And Jed was growing more and more interested in the gallery owner than might be good for either of them.

CHAPTER TEN

THE next morning Laura felt better about things. She rose early and quickly dressed in jeans and a loose top. She'd get the paintings and pen-and-ink drawings from Jed and find room for them in her workshop area. Heather could hold the fort for a while. Once back at the gallery, Laura would have to work to get another batch of paintings ready for sale. She was delighted the pictures had sold, and hoped the rest would find buyers.

Stopping at Callie's, she was surprised to find her already behind the counter.

"Don't you ever rest?" Laura asked.

"I could ask the same thing. What can I get you?"

"Breakfast for two again? I should have called, but this is a spur-of-the-moment decision. I'll have a cup of coffee while I wait."

By the time she turned on the road that led to the cottage, Laura felt like a teenage girl going on a first date. She could hardly wait to see Jed again. The burden of the opening night had lifted. The exhibit was going to be a success. Maria had seen the worst and dealt with it. Learned the truth and was going to have to find her own way to deal with that.

Now Laura wished she was strong enough to trust her instincts. She was uncertain about any future with Jed Brodie, but for once was going to quell those doubts and see what unfolded.

She had to park on the street as there was another car in the driveway beside Jed's. Laura didn't recognize it as one of the Brodies' vehicles. For a moment, she stayed in her car, indecision causing her to consider returning home and eating two breakfasts.

But it could be anyone, the cottage owner, a Realtor. Maybe she should find out who. Anyway, she and Jed had agreed upon nine this morning and it was already ten after. He was expecting her.

She lifted the basket Callie had prepared and headed for the front door. It was wide-open.

"Jed?" she called.

There was no response.

He wouldn't leave with the door open if he was going anywhere. Plus his rental car was in the driveway. Laura stepped inside. She put the basket down on the table near the sofa and headed for the studio. Maybe he'd started packing up the paintings.

As she neared the door, she could hear the murmur of voices, then silence.

She stepped into the room, stopping in shock. Tiffany had her arms around Jed's neck. They were kissing.

Déjà vu. She could see Jordan and Tiffany. Now Jed and Tiffany. Had their mother been right, what Jordan had, Jed wanted? For a moment she was frozen in place. The past could not be repeating itself. It wasn't fair!

She must have made a sound because Jed's hands came up and pulled Tiffany's arms down, stepping away and turning to look at Laura. Less than a second had passed, yet she felt as if the world slowed.

"Sorry. Guess I got my wires crossed," she said, spinning around and almost running out of the cottage.

"Laura, wait," he called behind her.

She could hear Tiffany say something, but not make out the words.

She didn't care. She just wanted to get away from the cottage and never return. It was definitely jinxed!

She opened the car door, but before it moved six inches, Jed slammed it shut, leaning against it. "You need to listen to me. It is not what it looked like."

"It looked like two people kissing. What part of that isn't what it looks like?" she asked. She refused to look at him. He was as big a betrayer as his brother. Why had she fooled herself that they could be different?

"She was kissing me," he said.

"Oh, I see, slender female overpowering muscular male. Yep, I get that picture. Not."

He put the edge of his hand beneath her chin and raised her face until her gaze met his. "I was not kissing Tiffany. She kissed me. Hell, she arrived at nine. I thought it was you when she knocked. I think she figures one brother is as good as the other."

Laura stared at him. Was he serious? Or was he trying to put an acceptable spin on things?

"Laura, there is nothing between me and Tiffany," he repeated.

"I do not think of you as Jordan," she repeated. "Yet you don't believe that. So why should I believe you?"

Jed dropped his hand and stepped back, his eyes narrowed as he regarded her for a long moment. "Impasse."

He glanced over at the cottage. Laura looked, as well, and saw Tiffany standing in the doorway. She sashayed down, her expression of satisfaction clear for all to see.

"See you later," she said, waving several fingers at Jed. With a smirk at Laura, she went to her car and got inside.

"Dammit!" Jed slammed a fist against the top of Laura's car. "I told you she was pure trouble."

Laura watched as Tiffany backed out. For a moment she felt a stab of hurt, then the smug look on the woman's face got to her. Was she deliberately causing trouble?

"Why?" Laura asked, turning back to look at Jed.

"She said I really reminded her of Jordan. One guy's as good as the next for her, I guess. Anyway, we could keep it all in the family, with her carrying my brother's baby and all. Since we are twins, we are the same DNA, so it would be like having the child's father."

Laura couldn't believe it. "Is she nuts?"

For a moment Jed held his breath. "I think so. Or mercenary. She has a better shot at the Brodie money if there's more than the baby involved." He watched Laura as she thought about the situation. He couldn't believe Tiffany had come on to him like that. If she'd loved his brother, as she claimed, he was not some stand-in.

But it wasn't Tiffany and his brother he was concerned about. It was this woman standing here. He knew Jordan had given her a rough time. Could she ever look at him and not see his twin? Ever look at him and see commitment and fidelity and not betrayal. How that scene must have replayed in her mind and seeing Tiffany with him had to cause her pain.

Without giving him a clue what she was thinking, she took her hand away from the door handle and turned toward the cottage.

"I brought breakfast. I didn't know if you'd had yours yet. It's probably cold by now. But I'm hungry. Then I need to get the paintings ready for pickup. Sally's friend Mike is supposed to be here this morning to transport them for me."

"I haven't had breakfast. And after the dramatics, I could use something. Did you bring any coffee?" Jed asked, walking with her up the walkway. Did she believe him or not? He'd known Tiffany's type the moment he saw her. She was so like Gwen in college. Jordan always ran true to form.

"I brought everything," she said.

She handed him the basket when he followed her into the cottage. He took it to the dining nook and opened it up. The carafe kept the coffee hot. The warming tray kept the food warm. This was the second time Laura had brought him breakfast. The first he understood—damage control. But why this morning?

She went to the kitchen and got out plates and eating utensils. In only a moment she set the table and sat in one of the chairs. The one she always used when she came before?

He didn't like the thought of her knowing more about the cottage than he did.

It was not something he'd admit to a living soul, but he was jealous of his brother and the relationship he had at one time with this woman. Jed wanted her to look at him with interest. With love.

Jed watched Laura as she began to eat. He took a bite. The omelet was light and fluffy and full of ham, cheese, mushrooms and scallions. A man could forget about working in the Amazon Basin if he had meals like this every day.

"About Tiffany," he began.

"No," Laura said. "You'll understand if I don't wish to discuss the woman. I can't think a single happy memory involving her."

"As long as you understand she was kissing me, not vice versa."

Laura inclined her head, concentrating on her breakfast.

Jed grew frustrated. He wanted her to say she believed him. That she knew he'd never be interested in anyone like Tiffany.

"She's not my type," he almost growled.

She looked up at that. "So you have a type?"

He'd just made things worse.

"No. I mean nothing about her appeals to me."

"It sure did to your brother."

"We are not alike for all we looked similar."

"Mmm," she said, reaching for the carafe of coffee and pouring herself a cup.

"And that means?"

"Jed, I know you and your brother are nothing alike. He was charming and knew how to sweep a woman off her feet. But he had no substance. Much as I thought I was in love with him,

I must have known deep inside that it wouldn't work. We never set a wedding date."

Jed didn't know how to take that bit of information. He almost winced when she said they were nothing alike and Jordan had been charming. So he wasn't charming. He'd known that all his life. He liked her comment about substance. She must think he had it if she continued the comparison.

Did that mean she didn't see him as a stand-in for his brother?

Yet when he'd kissed her, she'd called Jordan's name.

She studied him for a moment. Jed caught her gaze and regarded her with every appearance of confidence. But he wondered what she was thinking.

"You're planning to leave at the end of next week, right?" she said.

"Next Friday." Once the paintings were in her gallery and he finished sorting through Jordan's papers, there would be nothing holding him here. And the bridge wasn't going to build itself.

"How about we make a pact. I'll show you around Miragansett and the area, we'll make some memories together and neither one of us will ever mention Jordan or Tiffany."

That floored him. After all she'd witnessed today, she wanted to make memories together?

"Why?" he asked warily.

"Why not?" she countered.

"I can think of a couple of reasons. Humor me."

"Your career takes you far from this area. Who knows when you'll be back this way. I'd love for you to remember me when you're in the Amazon Basin, or bridging some raging river in Africa. And I still want those photographs. I was serious about that."

"Is this the gallery owner offering to keep a potential artist happy?" he asked.

She shrugged. "We could look at it that way if you want."

It was not the way he wanted to look at it. But it would give him six days with her without dealing with the ghost of Jordan between them. In that time surely he'd know if he could ever get past that ghost to form a lasting relationship with this woman.

Tiffany wasn't his type, but Laura could be.

"What do you have in mind?" he asked.

"I have to work today. Any chance you want to help me select the next batch of paintings to display?"

"I suggest you let my mother do that. I think it would help her to get involved."

Laura nodded. "Good idea. I'll call her as soon as I get to the gallery."

"No need. I have her number programmed into my cell phone." He withdrew it from his pocket and hit the speed dial number.

"Hello?" Maria answered.

"Mom? Jed here. Laura and I are having breakfast and she wanted to know if you'd help select the next batch of paintings for display."

"What are you talking about?" Maria asked.

"The paintings on display last night were sold out. Laura wanted to show some others and see if those would also sell."

"The paintings sold?" Maria asked.

"They were not up to your standards, but they weren't totally horrible," Jed said.

"Why are you and Laura having breakfast together?"

It was the opening he'd been hoping for. "We're seeing each other."

Laura dropped her fork and stared at him. Jed winked.

"I'll think about it," Maria said, and hung up.

"What are you thinking? You can't tell your mother something like that!" Laura said, glaring at him.

"Why not, I'm looking at you and seeing you, you're looking at me and seeing me. So we're seeing each other."

"You know what she'll think."

"So what?" he challenged.

"So—" She stopped and looked puzzled. "So I guess we just agreed to do that very thing."

Jed nodded in satisfaction. He was looking forward to the next six days.

By midafternoon all the paintings had been moved from the cottage and placed in the workshop. Laura had copies of the appraisals made to keep in the gallery, as well as the formal report she'd given Jed.

He'd helped until a few minutes ago, then disappeared.

"We can hardly turn around in here," Heather commented. She'd kept the gallery going while Laura had been moving the canvasses. Now she came into the workshop area to see what they had. "Um, I've had lots of requests today for more of these seascapes. Are we going to frame them first?" she said.

"We probably ought to offer the option. I hope I have enough frames. The exhibit is only for a few days. Any leftover inventory can then get framed later."

"Did I tell you two women today asked where they could contribute to the baby fund? They didn't want to ask you, being sure you'd be too devastated to respond. But they had heard about our fun and games of last night and wanted to help the poor new mother," Heather said.

"You're making that up," Laura said.

Heather shook her head. "I am not. I knew you'd be floored. Can you imagine anyone less in need of help than Tiffany? Good grief, most of the men here had to wipe the drool from their chins when she walked out. She'll be just fine."

"She was trying for Jed this morning," Laura said.

"Now you're making that up," Heather said with a laugh.

"Nope, walked in on a lip-lock that didn't quit."

Heather's amusement fled. "Are you sure he wasn't a willing partner?"

"He said not."

"And you believed him?"

Laura nodded. "I have to. I want him to believe me when I tell him something. I need to learn to trust unless I find out trust is not warranted." Instinctively she knew Jed was someone to depend upon. But her heart had a hard time believing that.

"I know he's yummy and all. And really more of a man if you know what I mean than his brother. But you're not falling for him are you?"

"Not really falling. Just—interested?"

"Because he looks like Jordan?"

"No! Why does everyone think that? He is a unique person. One I'm more attracted to than I was to Jordan. He's leaving soon and I may never see him again. I want the next few days to be perfect."

"What's happening the next few days?"

"I'm showing him around Miragansett."

"To make him fall in love with you?" Heather guessed.

Laura stared at her. Put that way, it was stupid beyond belief.

"You're right. How dumb can one person be?" she said.

"Hey, I didn't say anything about being dumb. Just think a minute. He doesn't live here on the Cape. He's working in Brazil. Do you know how far away that is? You can't open a gallery there. What are you going to do, see him Christmas and vacations? You're coming off a bad experience with Jordan. Don't ricochet to some other man. Take your time and find the right one."

Laura nodded, turning away. She was afraid Jed was the right one. Jordan had been the warm-up, Jed was the real thing. What was she going to do? She couldn't pack up and move, even if Jed asked her. Her life was here, and his wasn't.

Even if he felt the same way about her, they couldn't have a future together. There was too much between them. Not the least of which was Jordan Brodie.

CHAPTER ELEVEN

MONDAY morning dawned with scattered clouds. Laura dressed in shorts and a pullover cotton top, kept an eye on the sky. She and Jed were going sailing today, unless the weather made it impossible. She didn't take chances. If there was a storm brewing, they'd stay home.

But a few puffy clouds didn't necessarily mean a storm. She finished dressing and hurried into the kitchen to turn on the radio. The news was on. She half listened as she prepared breakfast, waiting for the weather. Finally the forecast. Scattered showers, possibility of thundershowers in late afternoon.

She went to the window and scanned the sky. They could still have a short sail and return before the storms blew up. She really didn't want to miss today. Their time together was rapidly drawing to a close.

Laura called Jed at seven-thirty.

"Brodie," he answered.

"Are you still game? There are scattered showers predicted this afternoon, but so far there's more blue in the sky than clouds."

"You're the captain, you call the shots."

Laura appreciated his vote of confidence. "Then I say we head out. If it starts to look threatening, we'll head for port."

"I'll meet you there at eight," Jed said.

Laura was already on the sailing boat when Jed arrived. She had everything packed away for lunch.

"Permission to come aboard, Captain?" Jed said from the dock.

"Permission granted," she said. When he stepped onboard, she reached up and gave him a kiss of welcome. She stepped back but he caught her around the waist and held her against him.

"Nice welcome, but you can do better than that," he said, lowering his mouth to hers and giving her a kiss that melted her knees.

A whistle from one of the other boaters in the marina broke them apart.

"Great, there goes my reputation," she murmured, laughing as she looked around to find the culprit.

"Or enhances it. What can I do?" Jed asked.

"Not a thing until we clear the marina. Then we'll hoist the sails and fly like the wind," she said, already blowing the engine compartment in preparation for starting the motor.

They had to watch out for the myriad of other boats already on the bay. Laura was a bit surprised to find so many boats on a Monday, but it was the height of the summer season and tourists and visitors abounded. She skillfully handled the boat and soon left the more crowded waters behind. The sun played peekaboo behind clouds. When shining it was hot.

"Know any places to swim?" Jed asked, sitting beside her and casually putting his arm around her shoulders.

"There are some more isolated beaches around the headland. The water's pretty cold."

"I remember from summers as a kid. But I came prepared in case we can swim."

"I have a swimsuit onboard. Sometimes the temperature climbs too high not to indulge," she said. "Want a turn steering?"

"Sure."

They changed places and she gave him a couple of pointers. He held the boat at the right angle to reap full benefit of the wind. They skimmed across the water, encountering only the mildest of swells. Clouds continued to gather overhead.

Laura took charge again when they approached the beach she wanted, though she felt Jed probably could have managed without any help from her. She headed for the one spot on the shore where she could get the boat in close. In no time they were anchored within a few yards of a pretty sheltered beach.

"We can swim and then eat," she suggested.

Jed agreed. He had his swimsuit on beneath his khakis. Laura had to change. She went to the small cabin and soon had on the abbreviated suit. Somehow it had not seemed so skimpy when she was swimming with Sally. She took a breath and flung open the door to step out on the deck.

Jed turned and let his gaze sweep over her, his smile showing appreciation.

"I could use some sunscreen," she said, offering the bottle of lotion. "If you could get my back, I can do the rest."

He took the bottle and poured the lotion in his palm, motioning for her to turn around. Laura had been trying to ignore the expanse of tanned chest inches away. Her fingers actually tingled in longing to rub against that warm skin. She longed to lean closer and breathe in his scent, touch him, feel the heat of his body against hers.

She turned and closed her eyes. They were going swimming, nothing more. They were seeing if they could become friends. That was a long way from what she wanted at this moment. Could they skip the preliminaries and get right down to it?

The lotion was cool against her skin, but his warm hand soon changed that. He carefully spread it over her shoulders, down her back, slipping beneath the narrow band of her bathing suit top to cover her skin. Lower, down her back to the top of the pants of the suit. Her heart raced. Her breathing seemed constricted. Every fiber of her being focused on the feelings Jed aroused in her. She felt alive, feverish, aware.

She needed to jump into that icy water right away!

"Now you can return the favor," he said.

She opened her eyes and turned, reaching for the suntan lotion. She poured some into her palm, put the bottle down and rubbed her hands together. He'd already turned, presenting that muscular back that was as tanned as any she'd seen.

"Doesn't look like you need it. Do you work without a shirt in the Amazon?"

"Sometimes. It's so humid there clothing sticks. I still wear sunscreen."

It was pure delight touching him as she'd dreamed about. She ran her hands over his back, feeling the strength of the muscles, the heat of his skin. He was rock-solid and masculine. She brushed the hair at his neck, making sure she covered every inch of skin. He felt so good. His back tapered toward his waist. She noted the difference in breadth as she ran her hands down along his spine, out around toward his ribs, back up across his shoulder blade.

"If you don't stop soon, I'm going to embarrass myself," Jed said in a low voice.

Laura pulled her hands back as if they'd been burned. She had long ago finished spreading the cream.

"All done," she tried to say brightly. Only her voice sounded husky and low.

Jed turned and looked at her. She met his gaze, knowing he'd see the hunger she couldn't hide.

He slowly reached out and drew her into his arms, pressing her closer as he began to kiss her. Almost every inch of her skin was touching his. Only the scanty scraps of material comprising their suits kept them apart.

His mouth moved against hers, demanding a response she was only too willing to give. His hand moved across her back, around to the front to cup her left breast, feeling it swell against his palm.

Laura gave a low moan of pleasure. She loved this man. Dare

she take such a risk again? Only, what choice did she have. Her heart was taken. The question now was what to do about that?

Slowly Jed ended the kiss finally resting his forehead against hers, looking into her eyes. "How far do you want to take this?"

She swallowed. All the way hovered on her lips, but she knew she would be rushing things. She wanted more than just an afternoon together.

"Maybe we stop now and take it up again later?" she suggested.

"Then let's go swimming," he said, turning to vault over the side of the boat.

His actions caught her by surprise. She rushed to the side to see him swimming toward the beach. She had to lower the ladder first so they could get back onboard, then finished putting the sunscreen on her arms and legs, all the while trying to get some control over her feelings. That kiss had been mind-blowing. She wouldn't mind another few thousands.

Finally she climbed down the ladder until she touched the water, jumping the rest of the way. The shock of cold took her breath away. She came to the surface and began to swim toward Jed. When a cloud blocked the sun, the water turned grey and felt even colder. She was glad to reach the shallows, it was warmer.

"This is great. I can't believe you knew a spot where there aren't a hundred tourists," he said, splashing toward her in the shallows.

She stood up and waded the rest of the way. "Sometimes there are families here, but more often than not, it's deserted. Sally found it first. We love to come here to sunbathe and swim and talk. If you climb the dunes, you'll see the forest comes right to the edge on the other side. I have no idea how to get here by land."

They explored the small beach, then swam some more in the shallows where the water was a bit warmer. The sun continued to appear and disappear. Jed stood and studied the sky at one point. Laura turned and saw the growing bank of dark clouds.

"I suggest we head back for the boat," she said. "Lunch and

then we head for home. I don't like sailing in storms—the wind and water are too unpredictable."

"Good idea. Race you." Without waiting for her agreement, he plunged into the water. She followed instantly, but knew long before she reached the boat that he could swim faster than she could.

As soon as they got onboard, Laura showed him the small shower to rinse off the salt water, then they dressed.

She brought out lunch and they ate on the bow, facing into the breeze and enjoying the rocking motion.

"A man could get used to this," Jed said, his eyes on the far horizon.

"One day I'd like to get a huge boat, and sail around America. There is so much to see from the Inland Passage to the Inter-coastal waterways. I think it would be great fun. Not that I see myself affording the boat or the time anytime soon. I'll probably have to wait until I'm too old to do it."

"Make plans to do it before you're too old. None of us know how long we'll be here. Don't wait too long," Jed said somberly.

"What is it you'd like to do that you've put off?" she asked.

He was quiet for a long moment. "Have a family, I guess. In the back of my mind was the thought that someday I'd get married, have some kids, a dog. Family gatherings where there's a lot of laughter and happiness. I missed that growing up. My parents were focused on their work. They shouldn't have had kids. They did their best, but I would want my family to be different."

Laura was intrigued to find out he wanted a family. Somehow, given his work, she never would have suspected.

"Would you expect your family to travel with you, or would you find a job closer to home?"

"There are plenty of jobs closer to home. I think a family should stick together, don't you?"

She nodded. "My family is close, except that my parents and

grandparents live in Iowa and don't know why I love the sea so much. They come to visit once a year and I go home for Christmas every year. I wouldn't trade anything about my childhood, except maybe to have a brother or sister."

"That can be overrated. Look at the situation with my brother."

"You must have had fun as children," she said.

He shrugged. "When we were young. But from the time we were teenagers, Jordan began pushing the limits. Always looking for an angle, a way to get around rules and regulations. And always after the girls."

"You mentioned when you first met Tiffany that this wasn't the first time. Did he get someone else pregnant before?" Laura asked. She'd wondered ever since Jed made that comment.

He nodded.

"Tell me," she said softly.

"We were almost finished our first year of college. He was in danger of being kicked out because of bad grades. He'd much rather party than study. And his idea of partying was seeing several different girls all at once. Sometimes as Jordan, sometimes as me."

"What?"

"A favorite pastime of his, fool people into thinking he was me."

"So what happened?"

"He got a girl pregnant, only he'd told her he was Jed Brodie. She came after me. She swore I was the one. I swore I had never met her before the day she and one of the assistant deans showed up at my dorm room. Jordan offered no help, blandly pretending he hadn't a clue what was going on. But the amusement he couldn't hide made me blow my temper."

"So did he fess up?"

"Only when one of my friends pointed out on several occasions the woman said she was with me, she was not because I was with Jim." Jed pointed to the area just beneath his left ear. "See this scar?"

She peered at it, a faint line about an inch long. "Yes."

"That's how Jim could tell Jordan and me apart. And he swore I was with him at soccer games when the alleged trysts took place. I think if Jim hadn't stood up for me, I would have been nailed as the father. Jordan fought, but lost. He ended up paying for the child's delivery expenses. The baby was given up for adoption."

"That's why you don't think he would have done right by Tiffany," she said slowly.

"Not unless it suited him. Jordan didn't have a very high sense of responsibility."

Laura gathered up the remnants of the meal and put them away in the bag she'd brought, then reached out and took Jed's hand, threading her fingers through his.

"I'm glad you stayed," she said, leaning against his shoulder and gazing out across the sea.

Jed would have sat like this for the rest of the day. Her hand was small in his, held loosely. Her weight leaning against his shoulder a pressure he could get used to. What would it be like to live in a locale like this, to be able to take off sailing whenever time permitted? He would have to rediscover how to relax. Most of his last few years were spent at job sites where the downtime didn't take a different turn from working.

"Much as I like this, we need to head back," Laura said, raising her head and frowning at the bank of dark clouds in the west.

"You fixed lunch, I'll take us to dinner. How about the Pelican again?"

"Sounds great." She smiled at him and it was all he could do to stop himself from sweeping her into his arms and taking up where they'd left off earlier.

Before they reached the marina, the rain began. It was not a bad storm as Jed thought of one at sea, with high winds and waves braking over the bow, just a steady drizzle of rain, soaking everything.

"Anything I can do?" he asked, standing beside her.

"Sorry about this, I thought we'd beat it back," she said.

"Hey, it's not like we didn't get wet swimming."

"But that was more fun than standing here. Aren't you cold?" She'd donned her clothes and an old windbreaker she'd had in the cabin. She offered him one that belonged to Sally, but he doubted it would fit.

"I'm not cold," he said. The rain was cool but after the months of heat in the Amazon, he reveled in it. If he got cold, he'd have to see about the jacket, but for now he felt exhilarated.

When they finally docked, Laura apologized again. He stopped her with a kiss.

"It was not dangerous. A little rain never hurt anyone. Stop apologizing."

"I wanted the day to be perfect."

"It was perfect."

"But the rain—"

He put his finger on her lips. "The weather wasn't perfect, but the shared experience was. I had fun, I think you did, as well. Isn't that what we wanted?"

She nodded.

"To build memories together," he said softly.

She seemed startled. Didn't she think he'd remember?

"They are as they are, but for us they'll forever be special."

She gave a shy smile.

"I'll pick you up at seven," he said, brushing his lips against hers again.

They walked back to their cars together and Jed watched as she drove off.

Another of their days together was almost gone. They had three more. Then he'd return to the Amazon Basin and work. And Laura would continue here in Miragansett.

Jed was already wondering if he could swing a trip home at

Christmas as he turned into the driveway of the cottage. Was he getting ahead of himself? Or just planning for the future?

His father sat on the porch. Jed was surprised to see him.

"Got caught in the rain?" Jefferson asked as Jed walked up in his wet clothes.

"Sure did. Come in. I'll change and be right with you."

"I'll fix something to drink," Jefferson said, heading for the kitchen.

Jed joined him a few minutes later, dry and warmer.

"I didn't expect you. I was sailing with Laura," Jed said when he entered the kitchen.

"She's a pretty thing, isn't she? Too good for Jordan. I never thought it would last. She wasn't bimbo enough for him."

Jed nodded. That described Jordan's girlfriends. He was surprised his father knew that.

"I came to see the pictures," Jefferson said.

Nothing was further from Jed's mind. He stared at his father for a long moment. "You did?"

"Laura had the right of it. We have a son we love. We need to learn more about him now that he's a man. Tell me about your work."

Jed knocked on Laura's door at seven. She opened it smiling at him.

"You are always on time. I like that," she said. "I'm ready."

"And I like that, no waiting around while you finish dressing."

She laughed and pulled her door closed. "I know, isn't that the dumbest thing. Where did that come from? I think punctuality is not rated high enough. You get dried out after the rain?"

"My father was at the cottage when I got there. He came to see my photographs. He only left a little while ago. Surprised me to see him there."

"Why? I'd think a parent would want to know about his child."

"First time."

"So, better than no time. Did he like them?"

"From an artistic point of view?"

"No, from learning more about what you do," she said as he opened the car door for her.

"He had lots of questions. I think he left knowing more what I do, and why."

"That's what parents should do."

"Do yours?"

"Heavens, yes. My mother is always giving me advice on how to better display paintings, and what carpeting to get next. Dad offers help in a balcony garden if I wanted to grow my own vegetables."

"Did they meet Jordan?"

She shook her head.

"Why not?"

"They are coming out in a couple of weeks. At the time I got engaged, I thought there was no rush. Then later, I was glad they hadn't."

Jed wondered what Laura's parents were like. He'd heard meeting a person's parents could give someone an idea of what that person would be like in thirty years. He hoped that wasn't strictly true. He did not want to be like either of his parents, now or in the future.

"I hope you are planning on dancing," Laura said. "I wore my dancing shoes."

"Why else go to the Pelican?" he responded. Tonight was for the two of them.

The days flew by. Tuesday Laura took off from work and they went clamming—ending up with a group of her friends at a big clambake on the beach. Only one or two people mistakenly called Jed Jordan. The rest welcomed him as he was and had no trouble keeping his identity straight.

Wednesday Laura and Jed drove to Provincetown and went

antique shopping. She was looking for some old display cases to incorporate in her gallery, but found nothing she wanted. Still, the time together was what counted. And Jed was as interested in the history of some of the antique pieces of furniture as she was.

Thursday she had to meet with some artists and a serious collector. They caught a matinee at the local theater, enjoying a romantic comedy together.

That night they ate dinner at her flat.

Tomorrow Jed was leaving for Brazil.

CHAPTER TWELVE

LAURA had the table set with candles, her best china and silverware. The wineglasses sparkled in the flickering light. The rest of the apartment shone. She had made sure his last evening would be special. For dinner she was having clam chowder, lobster and crusty French bread. His mother hadn't provided his favorite meal, but Laura would.

Nothing had been said about a future. Would he bid her farewell tonight and head back to work and forget about her within the week?

"Maybe not that soon, but will he come back to see me? Somehow discover he can't live without me?" she said aloud, already feeling blue that he was going.

She sank on the sofa and gazed out the window. Rain was again predicted. They couldn't even take a last walk along the beach or around town. After dinner, he'd thank her for the meal and leave. Return to the hotel where he'd moved yesterday after winding up the last of Jordan's affairs and closing the cottage. It would be rented to someone else within days.

Laura wasn't sorry to know she'd never go there again. But she didn't like the finality of everything.

He knocked, right at seven. She could set her watch by him.

She rose and crossed to the door, smiling for joy at seeing

him. Hoping the sadness that threatened to overwhelm her would remain at bay until he left tonight.

"For you," Jed said, flourishing a bouquet of colorful flowers. Their fragrance filled the entryway.

"They're beautiful." She swallowed hard, blinking to keep the tears at bay. She hadn't been given flowers many times in her life. How sweet he'd give her some today. A farewell gift. She refused to think about it.

"Let me get them in some water."

He followed her into the kitchen as she found a vase and filled it with water. The arrangement was lovely. She placed them in the center of the table, moving the candles a little.

He came over and drew her into his arms, kissing her gently.

"I have your favorite for dinner," she said a minute later, pushing away lest she grab hold and never let go.

"You cooked lobster?"

She laughed. "Once again Callie came to the rescue. She prepared everything. I have it all warming. I wanted your last night here to be special."

"Do you like lobster?"

"I love it. But I don't cook it. Too traumatic."

He smiled at the face she made. Plunging live lobsters into boiling water was not her idea of cooking. She much preferred Callie do the awful deed. Laura liked to think her lobster came from the supermarket neatly wrapped in cellophane, not live from the sea.

"Are you all set to leave?" she asked.

"Packed and ready. I'll have to go early in the morning to get to Logan Airport in time for the flight. I'll turn in the rental car there," Jed said calmly.

The least he could do was look remorseful, or regretful or somehow sad, she thought, feeling the minutes fly by. Only a couple of hours and she'd have to say goodbye. She wasn't ready.

For a moment her throat closed up. There was so much more to say, but she felt tongue-tied.

"This is delicious," Jed said as he ate the chowder. "Rich and flavorful."

"Callie's a great cook. Sadly I'm not. It's not worth it to cook much for one. When I have friends over, we usually all bring something, more like a potluck. I eat out a lot."

She was babbling. She'd already told him that earlier in their relationship.

"At least you have the choice. For us it's the company's chow line or nothing," Jed said.

"I guess you make up for it when you hit a city."

"First stop is always a fine restaurant. Or the bar, for some guys."

"You're excited to be going back, aren't you?"

"I've missed several weeks. Never been away from a job like that before."

"Will you take time off at Christmas?"

He was silent for a moment, studying her. "Will you be here at Christmas?"

"No, Iowa." Should she invite him there? "We're sure to have snow. Want to come?"

He shook his head. "With any luck we'll be in the final stages of construction. That's summer there and we work long hours while daylight is plentiful."

"What about Jordan's estate?"

"I think I've got everything lined up. The attorney knows what I want. It's just a question of winding up the legal work. If the DNA testing shows Tiffany's baby is Jordan's, and I believe her, I'll set up a trust for the child. I'm not giving the money to her, but put my father and the attorney as trustees to see to the baby's welfare. I've given the attorney my e-mail address, so he can contact me immediately if anything else comes up. And he said he'll fax any paperwork I need to sign.

Which reminds me." He reached into his pocket and pulled out a card, putting it on the table near Laura.

"Contact information. In case you want to write or something."

She reached for the card, a stupid smile plastered on her face. She was fighting tears. In case she wanted to? Try and stop her. If that's all they had for the foreseeable future, she'd make the most of it.

"I'm taking one of the programs from the gallery back with me, it has your e-mail address on it," he said.

"You'll be going back to winter," she said.

"Winter in the Amazon is not much different from summer, except for shorter days. Still hot and humid. Will you write?"

She nodded, blinking to keep the tears at bay. "Sure. I'll let you know how the sketches sell, and what your mother is doing and—"

"Mostly I want to know what you're doing," he interjected.

"I'll be working at the gallery."

"And sailing, going to clambakes. Discovering new talent. I want to hear it all."

"Why?"

"I like this slice of life you have for yourself, Laura. When I'm lying on my bunk sweltering in the heat, I can read about your sailing in the cool waters off the Cape. Or up to your knees in the Atlantic digging clams."

"So you need to write me about how the bridge is going. And send me pictures. I'll get them printed and see what sells."

They discussed options for Laura's branching out into a different facet of art with photographs. She considered opening a satellite office with a separate name, which would offer art more suited to the average tourist. The more she thought about it, the more excited she became. She had to focus on something or her heart would break with Jed's leaving.

She broached the idea to Jed and was surprised to get his wholehearted approval. They discussed the ramifications, where she should locate the shop, start-up costs and other aspects. Before she knew it the meal was over.

It was growing late…it was already dark outside. She wasn't ready. Why couldn't she make time stand still!

"Thanks for the dinner, it was delicious," Jed said when he finished. He put his napkin on the table and pushed back his chair. "I need to get going. I have to get up early for my flight."

She nodded. After all, what was left to say?

Laura walked him to the door. He turned and took her into his arms, kissing her gently, on the mouth, the forehead, the cheeks.

"I'm glad I got to know you, Laura."

"Don't go," she said involuntarily. Her eyes were swimming in tears as she tried to see him clearly, imprint his image on her mind forever.

"I have to. Who knows, in a few months or a year, I might be back. And we could see what we have."

"I know what I have. You're the one who won't trust me," she whispered.

"Ah, honey, don't." He pulled her against his chest, rubbing his hand over her back, cradling her head against his chest. "I remind you of Jordan. I've always known that."

"You're stupid like he was if that's what you believe. You don't remind me a bit of Jordan," she said, muffled against him. She could stay here forever.

"All my life I've battled to be my own person," he said. "Jordan loved playing up the twin feature, I wanted to downplay it."

She pulled back enough to see him. "He's gone, Jed. I'm sorry for his death. He wasn't the man for me, but he didn't deserve to die so young. However, I do *not* see him when I look at you. You're strong and honorable and successful. You don't blame others for your actions or depend on others to exist. You love your parents even when they don't deserve it. You are dependable and compassionate. You know what's right and do it, no matter what the personal cost. I love you. I'll never forgive myself for the words murmured when I wasn't thinking, but I never once in all the time I've known you confused you with your brother. He's the unfinished version. You're complete. Go off to South America. Build your bridge. But when you're done, come back here and see me. See if you can find the love in you that burns so brightly in me. I want you. I want the home and kids and dogs and love that you and I together could have."

"You tempt a man. Maybe in a year or two. When you've forgotten him."

"Well, you tell yourself that, pigheaded man. I want you now. And I'm sure I'll want you in a year or two or ten. Is that what it'll take? Being faithful to only you for a decade before you'll trust me?"

"It's not that," he said.

"What then?"

"My mother had it wrong. Jordan and I didn't compete for the same girls in high school or college—what would be the point? I couldn't compare with his charming ways. If I was interested in a girl, he'd saunter over and before you knew it, she was falling beneath his spell. No competition."

"You never waited around long enough for them to fall out from beneath the spell, I bet. Then they see the dross instead of the gold. With you, it's all gold."

He kissed her. "Hold that thought. I'll write."

He was gone before she could react.

She stared at the door for a long time, gradually realizing despite everything she'd said, he still didn't believe her. He'd left.

Laura didn't move for the longest time, convinced he'd knock on the door, tell her he'd been an idiot and confess he loved her. She thought he did. The last few days had been heavenly. They had so much in common, and when they'd disagreed, they ended up laughing at the absurd lengths they'd go to in order to make their point. She could see them together in five years, ten, forty. Something she never saw with Jordan.

Finally she moved, dazed. He wasn't coming back.

She cleared the table, did the dishes, all as if in a fog.

When it was time for bed, she knew she wouldn't sleep. She grabbed her duvet and went out on her balcony. It was cool, the evening breeze damp from the sea. Wrapping up warmly, she sat in her chaise, gazing at the tiny sliver of water blurred by the evening mist.

If she could live over one minute of her life it would be the one where she'd said Jordan's name when another man kissed her. One small thing which apparently was going to haunt her forever.

Jed drove back to the hotel, parked and got out. The evening mist gave everything a surreal look. It was not going to dampen his mood. He was too keyed-up to go to bed, so opted for a last walk through town. He had gotten to know some of Miragansett while he'd been here. It was a nice place. He'd like to come back in the off season and see what it was like then.

Laura would be here, unless she was on one of her buying trips.

Her words of love echoed in his mind. He wished he believed her. She was right, he didn't. Was he to battle the specter of his brother all his life? He was a grown man. Jordan was gone.

If he'd met Laura without her knowing Jordan, he would never doubt her.

The sound of his brother's name on her lips when he kissed her echoed. Was he doomed to forever be second to his brother?

It was cool, but the damp air cleared his head. Gradually he began to think of the days ahead. He had the work at the bridge site to keep him busy. If she wrote, he'd write back. Maybe as he said, when he came back to the States, he'd come to see her again.

He wanted to turn around right now and storm back to her flat and tell her—tell her what? That he loved her even if she loved his brother?

All thoughts led back to Laura.

Finally growing tired, Jed returned to the hotel

Her words of love echoed in his mind. The first time anyone had put him ahead of Jordan. Was it only because Jordan was no longer around?

For the first time in his life, Jed listened to the words, and believed them. He had made a success of his life. He wasn't dependent on his parents, didn't flit from woman to woman without a thought of responsibility or duty. He didn't manipulate people. And Laura said she loved him.

Could he believe that?

The woman had a sterling reputation in town for being honest as the day is long. He'd heard plenty of comments the night of the opening.

Dare he take a chance? He knew Laura would make him happy. Could he make her happy?

I work in South America, in case you hadn't noticed, he argued with himself.

Could he trust Laura? It came down to that.

The pounding on the door woke her. It was dark outside. Laura rose groggily and went to see if there was an emergency.

Jed stood there.

"What's wrong?" she asked.

He stepped inside and kissed her. "My car is downstairs, I'm on my way to the airport. But I didn't sleep at all last night. I can't leave for Brazil without telling you I love you. I want you, too. Let's get married. As soon as I get back? I'll take what I can get and spend the next fifty years or so making you the husband you want."

"Wait a minute. Is this a proposal? You'll take what you can get?" she asked, heart pounding. It was what she wanted, just not the way she wanted it.

"I want you."

"Repeat after me, I believe you, Laura. You love me best."

He smiled. "I believe you, Laura, you love me best, and it had better stay that way forever!"

With a whoop of joy, Laura encircled his neck and pulled him down for a kiss.

"Is that a yes?" Jed asked a minute later.

"Yes, of course it's a yes. I love you."

"I love you. Marry me as soon as I get back from this assignment?"

"Yes. Wait, how long is that going to be?"

"Another eight or nine months, enough time to get everything lined up."

"And for you to miss most of the wedding planning."

"We'll be linked electronically. Say yes, sweetheart, I have to catch that plane."

She hugged him tightly. "Don't go."

"I have to, but I'll be back, and then we'll find that house together and start on our family."

"What about bridges?"

"Don't they need them in America?"

"I guess."

"I can build other things, as well. Don't worry, you won't starve."

"Silly, I'm not worried about that. I want you doing what you want."

"I will. And find a way to mesh our lives so I'm not out of the country while you're having our babies. I love you. Take a chance on me."

"I love you, Jed. There's no chance to take, only a blissful future."

He kissed her again.

"What changed your mind?" she asked breathlessly a few moments later.

"Jordan."

"How?"

"He died. What if I died and never knew what being married to you could be like? What if you died before I could tell you I loved you? Life's too uncertain to let things stall. I love you and am willing to put it right out there for all the world to know," he said.

"I plan to live to a hundred, just so you know," she said, hugging him tightly.

"Those match my own plans. Wait for me. I'll be back as soon as I get the bridge built."

"I'd wait until the end of time, Jed. I love you!"

The kiss he gave her had to last a long time. It almost did!

EPILOGUE

Fifteen months later

"ARE you ready?" Jed asked, coming into the bedroom.

"Almost. What time is it?"

"Just after six."

"Yikes, we'll be late."

"They won't start without you."

"I can't be late on the opening night of the new gallery. I have a reputation to make in this town."

"Ride on your reputation from Miragansett," he said, leaning against the doorjamb and watching his wife of six months put the finishing touches on her makeup. He would never tire of watching her. She was beautiful. He wanted to kiss that lipstick off and take her to bed. But this was her big night and he was celebrating with her.

"Boston is an entirely different venue. No one here cares about Miragansett."

"Too bad, I like the place."

"Which is why we bought that house there. But Boston is home now."

"Except for weekends when we head for the Cape. Heather is a perfect manager."

"She was thrilled, wasn't she? I'm glad Callie is catering this event tonight. I don't want anything to go wrong."

"Nothing will. My parents checked in earlier today, I talked to my father."

"I can't believe their support—your mother and your father using my new gallery exclusively. Along with recommendations to several of their colleagues. With that kind of material, how can it fail?"

"It can't, but that's because of you, sweetheart, not the artwork you acquired."

She set down her brush, examined herself one last time then turned and walked to Jed. Reaching up, she kissed him.

"You're okay with working here in Boston?" she asked. He'd just received a new construction project, a high-rise office building near the downtown area.

"Yes." She asked him that almost daily. He'd known what he was doing when he accepted the project. The months at the bridge site after proposing had seemed endless, even with the two or three e-mails a day from Laura. They'd grown to know each other well through their correspondence, but nothing beat being with her. He'd change careers before taking off again for months without her.

"Are you okay with living here instead of by the sea?" he asked.

"Boston's by the sea. I'll go to the quay anytime I need a salt water fix. I'm building an empire, you know. With the gallery in Miragansett, the second shop that caters to tourists and now this one, I'll be a mogul in no time."

"If anyone deserves it, it's you. Don't stop. Why not a place in New York, as well."

She laughed. "Now you're dreaming. Let's get to the gallery. I have some news to share with you later."

"And that is?"

"Later, I said. You're all right with your parents staying at the hotel? We could have had them here," she said.

"Dad and I get along fine. But for mother, I'll always be second to Jordan."

Laura reached out to touch his arm. "You'll always be first to me," she said.

"It was nice of her to give us that painting she did after Jordan died for a wedding present—with the caveat you sell it." he said. "Any nibbles?"

"It's the centerpiece of tonight's exhibit. I've priced it exorbitantly. If it sells, it'll be a miracle. But it is wonderful. Just having it in my gallery will give us the cachet we need to be taken seriously."

"Not to mention Dad's sculptures."

"Wasn't that a coup? Wonder why he did that—switched to me exclusively, I mean."

"To keep it all in the family. Which reminds me, prepared to be bored with a million pictures of little Jordie. Mother carries around an album and is always updating the photos."

"Grandmothers should dote on their grandchildren. I'm just glad Tiffany lets him visit them."

Jed kept quiet about the deal he'd made with the woman. As long as she allowed Jordie to visit his grandparents, Jed supplemented the trust fund. Even though most of Jordan's paintings and a good portion of the pen-and-ink drawings had sold, so far the entire estate had not amounted to a great deal, divided as it had been. Jed's share had gone to Jordie's trust, as well. And he suspected his mother and father slipped the woman some money. He was fine with that. The little boy looked a lot like Jordan.

Laura looked up at him with mischief in her eyes. "I was going to wait, but maybe I don't want to. We want equal time Maria and Jefferson will soon be grandparents a second time I'm hoping for a girl, what about you?"

Jed looked at her, surprise and delight sweeping through him. "We're pregnant?"

"Due in seven months!"

He swept her up and spun her around. "Married six months and now we're going to be parents. Hot damn!"

She smiled at his happiness. Jed knew then he'd made the right decision that night. Some risks were meant to be taken. Every day he knew he came first with Laura. And every day he gave thanks for the gift of her love.

"Guess you know what this means," she said.

"What?" A new place to live—a house with a yard. Telling his parents. Telling hers. Would they wait for the Christmas visit?

"We need to decide the issue of art lessons. Personally I'm against them," she said, teasing. "I want us to be a happy family with no favorites and no stress about following in footsteps. Each child goes his or her own way!"

"Deal!"

She laughed at his agreement, knowing he was happy. She gave thanks every day for his coming into her life. Only when reminded by Maria or Jefferson did she give any thought to the young man she'd once been engaged to. He was so far removed from her husband she never understood how she could have been fooled into thinking she loved him. When the real thing appeared, she knew the other had been nothing, a girl's first venture into infatuation.

"I love you, Laura," Jed said softly.

"I love you, Jed, always and forever." Her vow was sealed with a kiss.

* * * * *

Every Life Has More
Than One Chapter™

Award-winning author Stevi Mittman delivers another
hysterical mystery, featuring Teddi Bayer, an irrepress-
ible heroine, and her to-die-for hero, Detective Drew
Scoones. After all, life on Long Island can be murder!

*Turn the page for a sneak peek
at the warm and funny fourth book,
WHOSE NUMBER IS UP, ANYWAY?,
in the Teddi Bayer series,
by STEVI MITTMAN.
On sale August 7*